Don't Waste The Years

*To Sharna
thanks for
your support.

L. Lewis*

Don't Waste The Years

Lavern Lewis

Copyright © 2012 by Lavern Lewis.

Library of Congress Control Number: 2012919860
ISBN: Softcover   978-1-4797-3831-1
           Ebook   978-1-4797-3832-8

All rights reserved. No part of this book may be reproduced or transmitted in any form or by any means, electronic or mechanical, including photocopying, recording, or by any information storage and retrieval system, without permission in writing from the copyright owner.

This is a work of fiction. Names, characters, places and incidents either are the product of the author's imagination or are used fictitiously, and any resemblance to any actual persons, living or dead, events, or locales is entirely coincidental.

Book cover was done by Orville Robinson

This book was printed in the United States of America.

Rev. date: 07/10/2013

To order additional copies of this book, contact:
Xlibris LLC
1-888-795-4274
www.Xlibris.com
Orders@Xlibris.com
120505

ACKNOWLEDGMENTS

FIRST OF ALL I would like to thank God for blessing me with the ability to get these characters out of my head. I would like to dedicate this book to my parents Agatha and Beresford Lewis. To my kids Shane, Anthony and Anika; as well as my beautiful grandkids Jahni, Jahzi, Akailah and Jalen. I would also like to thank Leanna McGrath and Marsha Syblis for putting up with me and still giving me their support. A heartfelt thank you goes out to Mr. R.T. for being in my life at a time when I really needed someone. Words can't even begin to express how much I love you and I only wish that I had met you earlier on in my life. Last but not least, I would like to thank everyone else that has believed in me and couldn't wait to read my book.

DON'T WASTE THE YEARS

Dear Reader,

    While writing this book I wanted to put a face to each of my main character, a face that my readers could also relate to. So, as you read each page allow your imagination to be free and envision these actors playing the roles of:

Howard ~ Terrence Howard
Vanessa ~ Sanaa Lathan
Rachel ~ Taraji P Henson
Omar ~ Morris Chestnut
Lorrain ~ Gabrielle Union
Steveroy ~ Terrance J
Kim ~ Regina Hall
Richard ~ Lamman Rucker
Tracy ~ Megan Good
Dmitri ~ Michael Ealy
Tyrone ~ Brain J. White
Leroy ~ Mike Epps
Mike (bartender) ~ Pooh Hall
Howard's mom ~ Angela Bassett
Howard's dad ~ James Picker Jr.
Mr. Edwards ~ Keith David
Mrs. Bedford ~ Loretta Divine

'My Imperfections Are What Makes Me Who I Am . . . SimplyMe'.

SEXUAL FIX

THE NEXT THING she knew, she was on her knees undoing his pants. She took every inch of his erection into her mouth as her hand moved up and down his shaft. As good as it felt he didn't have time for that; he pulled her up, spun her around and lifted her dress. Just then he remembered that he no longer carried a condom in his wallet.

"Please tell me you have protection?" he asked.

"No, but just put it in."

There was no going back now because he had to have her so; he entered her without any protection. He forcefully put ever inch of his harden manhood inside, then he pounded her from behind like a piece of meat that needed to be tenderized, while holding onto her hair. She moaned which aroused him but he wasn't ready to come yet so, he pulled out and told her to get on the couch. While on her back Tracy reached up to kiss him but he turned his head instead.

"No kissing just fucking because I only kiss my wife." As she laid there she felt hurt by his words but she knew this was the only way she could ever have him and for tonight it was good enough. He didn't care if he was hurting her because it was all about what he wanted as he continued fucking her. He then opened her legs as far as they would go so, that he could go deeper with every stroke. Howard felt every inch of his body exploded as he released his entire load inside of her. Tracy wanted him to re-enter her but instead he grabbed the back of her head and rammed his still hard manhood as far as it would go into her mouth. He noticed that she wasn't gagging like she used to, as he fucked her face and then released in her mouth.

"It looks like someone has mastered the art of deep throat" he said.

CHAPTER ONE

WHEN HOWARD TERRENCE Blackwood found out that his time was limited he decided it was time to write his Will. He walked into the building with a whirlwind of thoughts ripping him apart. As he rode the elevator to the twenty-five floor he thought about his friendship with his lawyer. Raymond Boston was a long time friend, they worked together as a janitor after he moved out of Tracy apartment. Throughout the years they had always kept in close contact with each other. If it wasn't for Raymond breaking his leg, Howard would have never met his wife Vanessa at the hospital. From the moment he saw her, he was mesmerized by her beauty and he knew that he wanted her to be a part of his life. Vanessa was doing her internship at the hospital that night, while Howard waited for Raymond to get his cast on. She was being trained on how to use the computer system. As she tried to concentrate on the instructions the nurse was giving her; she could feel him staring at her. Every so often she would look up at him and smile because she thought he was cute. Before leaving the hospital Howard slipped her a note with his name and number that read. "I would love to get to know you. Give me a call please". Three weeks later she finally called him.

When Howard entered the office, he was informed by the receptionist that Raymond was in with a client. After a twenty minute wait the door opened and an elderly woman walked out, followed by Raymond. He gave her a kiss on her forehead and told her that she was in good hands as she walked off. He then looked in Howard's direction.

"Are my eyes deceiving me or is that really Howard Blackwood?"

"It hasn't been that long since we've seen each other. I was just at your wedding?" As they continued to talk Raymond gestured for him to follow him into his office; he closed the door behind them and sat behind his desk while Howard remained standing.

"Now Howard, how long has it been since I've married, or have you forgotten?"

"Okay. No need to get technical about it, I'm here now."

"So, what brings you into my neck of the woods?"

"Well I need you to prepare a Living Will for me as soon as possible."

"Why is there something wrong?"

"I really don't have the time to get into it, but I will let you know when the time is right. Here is all of the information I think you will need but if there is anything else just let me know."

"So, that's it; you're not going to tell me anything else are you?"

"No, not right now, I have to get to work but I'll call you."

Before Raymond could say another word, Howard was on his way out the door and his next appointment was waiting in the lobby. Raymond respected Howard very much and was worried as to why he would want him to write his Will. Considering he wasn't even forty yet. While greeting his next client Raymond gave himself a mental note to call Howard later that evening to find out what was really going on.

As Howard left the office he couldn't help but wonder why this was happening to him. Throughout his life he had struggled to get the things he wanted and needed but he was confident that he had finally reached a place in his life where he was financially comfortable. Coming from Jamaica at the tender age of two he felt that he had lost out on his Jamaican culture. In the process of giving him a better life his parent's Howard Sr. and Sylvia stole from him all that would have made him a better man. His father was a very strict man that ruled his household with an iron fist and in order to live under his roof his wife and kids had to go by his rules. He was an old fashion man that felt that he should take care of his family financially. There was only one job his wife should have, which was taking care of the household. Howard had no respect for the way his father treated his mother and although he would never laid a hand on her; the way he spoke to her was just as damaging. His mother did as she was told and was always scared to speak whenever he was around. There was nothing Howard could do that was right in his father's eyes. When his grandfather passed the family business onto his father because his uncle was a drug addict; his father felt it was his duty to do right by his father. However, he never realized how hard it would be to run BGR (Blackwood Garbage Removal). After a hard day of trying to fill his father's shoe he would come home and take all of his frustration out on his wife and kids. For three years Howard was forced to go to work with his dad and although he did get paid it wasn't something he enjoyed doing. Even when he was seventeen his father restricted him from becoming his own person. With a savings of two thousand and ten dollars Howard left home with all that he could carry in hope of a more fulfilling life. Having nowhere to go he decided to stay with a friend until he could figure out what his next step would be. He continued to go to school which was something that he promised his mother he would do, the day he left home. It was hard for him to leave his mother and two sisters' but they knew that he would always keep in touch with them. They also knew that he would never return home as long as his father was there. He called plenty of times to speak with his mother and sisters but he would never accept any of his mother's offers to give him money because he knew it was his father's money. His father would occasionally answer the phone but he never asked how he was doing, if he needed anything or for him to return home. When Howard's father realized that his only son didn't want to take over the family business he disowned him. He couldn't understand why Howard thought that he was too good to take over the business, in which his grandfather had built from the ground up; a business that had fed and clothed him. His father knew that one of his daughters could take over the business but he felt that Howard should be the one. However, that's not what Howard wanted to do with his life.

He spent two months with his friend Peter but felt it was time to leave after his girlfriend moved in. After spending a few nights on the streets Howard then decided to stay in a shelter. He was now struggling to keep up with his homework because all he could think about was how he was going to pay for his upcoming college tuition fees. However when he bumped into Tracy Williams two weeks later and knocked her groceries out of her hands everything changed for him. She lived on her own and was one of the highest paid strippers at the Big Sexy Night Club. The following week Howard was living with her and she was taking care of all of his expenses. All he had to do was stay with her at the club every night and make sure she got home safely. Although he was only seventeen his age was never questioned because of his size. Their relationship was strong, she helped him with his studies while he made sure that no one crossed the line at the club. Tracy wasn't Howard's first sexual encounter but she taught him a lot about pleasing a woman considering she constantly wanted sex. Many times she would remind him that she was paying the bills and he was at her beck and call. Her sexual desires were taking a toll on his body because she wanted to have sex two sometime three times a day; which left him with little time to keep up with his studies. It wasn't because he didn't enjoy having sex with her or because he couldn't keep up; it was just that he needed to focus on his finals and Tracy was a major distraction. She was a very demanding woman when it came to her sexual needs. Many times after having sex she would still masturbate not because he couldn't satisfy her; it's just that she needed to finish herself off. For as long as she could remember she always loved to masturbate. She would pretend that it was her lover pleasing her instead of the store bought substitute that wasn't as pleasurable without the batteries. She even admitted to Howard that she loved to be fucked but not every man could satisfy her the way she needed to be. Many have tried and failed but there has been a handful that has succeeded. After living with Tracy for two years Howard found out that it wasn't as easy pleasing her because she was a very needy person and would lash out when things didn't go her way. With Tracy's sexual appetite she needed several men to please her because she was never satisfied. If Howard continued to pleasure her as often as she needed it; she would be the death of him. While living with her, Howard decided to put half of the money she gave him into his savings account because he knew that it was only a matter of time before she got on his last nerve. If it wasn't for her money and the great sex he would never have been in a relationship with a woman like her because she was selfish and inconsiderate when it came to his needs; even if she always made him laugh.

    A year later when Howard found out that Tracy was doing much more than just stripping to make her money his feeling for her changed. He could no longer sleep with her knowing that other men were paying her for sex. Howard tried many times to convince her that she was better than that and she should stop stripping but no matter what he said it didn't work. It made him sick to his stomach when one of her customers reminded him how much he was paying for her services.

    Tracy thought by threaten to cut him off he would agree to have sex with her again. However, knowing that his tuition fee was already paid for; Howard took the money he had saved to rent a small one bedroom apartment until he was able to find a steady job. After finishing his three year apprenticeship program he was a Certified Carpenter and when he was hired at Lewis & Son Cabinetry he quit his job as a janitor.

CHAPTER TWO

AFTER HOWARD LEFT her, Tracy had a hard time moving on because she didn't realized how much she loved him until he was gone. She knew that he was right she needed to do something more with her life so she took classes during the day and worked at night. Once she was finish school she got a job at Profitable Investments Publishing Company as the receptionist. It was a self publishing company that work with individuals that wanted to publish their own book; while allowing people to invest in affordable packages that would best suit their financial needs to get their book published. Within four years of starting off as the receptionist, she then moved to sales, from there the editing department until she became the manager of editing. So when the company was expanding and was looking for someone to lead the editing department for their new location; there was no doubt that she would be a perfect fit even though there were several others people that had applied for the position.

It was never important for Tracy to have a car because when she was with Howard she had bought him one to take her to work and before that she would just take a cab. However now that she would be working downtown at the new location she would have to take the bus to work which sucked. She was thrilled that the company was giving her a new car; she just needed to get her licenses renewed. On her first day of work she missed the bus and arrived ten minutes late, but was glad to know that her boss was also running late. When she arrived Tammy the receptionist showed her to her new office. For the past four years she had worked her ass off and now as she looked around her office she knew that all of her hard work had paid off. They gave her, her own office, a three year contract, a company car (which she would be picking up at the end of the day) and to top it off she now made eighty thousand a year. Tracy walked over to her desk and sat in her new chair, everything in her office was new because the company had recently renovated to make room for her office. Although it was smaller than what she had expected: it still had a big ass desk, built in bookcase, two chairs, a large window and a sofa. As she spun around in her chair thoughts of Howard ran through her mind, she would love for him to see her now. She still loved him but he was a married man now and her love for him scared her because he was just another man that she knew she could never have to herself. Just then Antoinette the office manager knocked on the door and brought her out of her thoughts.

"Come in!"

"Good morning Ms. Williams. How do you like your new office?"

"Now Antoinette you know you can call me Tracy. As for the office it's great."

"Ok Tracy; well if there is anything else that you need just let me know?"

"I just love the view and I didn't realize that I would be getting all new furniture."

"Yes we decide to go all out for you; not only because you've earned it but you are very valuable to the company and you deserved it."

"Thanks Antoinette that means a lot to me."

"No need to thank me it's the truth. Now here is a list of your daily duties. I've assigned you to work on Mr. Beresford's new book, so you will be working with him directly and keep in mind he is one of our most difficult clients to work with. However if you can handle him you will not only prove to us that we've hired the right person but it will also mean that we won't have to babysit you. Now if you follow me I'll show you where you can find everything."

They left her office and for the next two hours Antoinette showed Tracy where everything she needed would be, as well as all the passwords and the access pass for the ladies restroom that would only be used by five other employees. The new location was much bigger and had over one hundred employees. They then had lunch with the other editors, where Tracy was able to meet Jennifer the last person who was assigned to work with Mr. Beresford. She describe him as a wealthy distinguish black ladies man, that likes to get his own way and liked to raise his voice but she shouldn't take it personal because that's just the way he talked and if he feels that your intimidated by him; he will walk all over you.

As Jennifer continued talking Tracy felt as if she should be taking notes with all the information that was being given. By two o'clock she was back in her office and although she wanted to look over Mr. Beresford's book, Antoinette had instructed her to read her e-mail and reply as soon as possible. Once her e-mail was opened she noticed that there was over thirty, the first one read "Please pick-up your Nissan Maxima 3.5 SE today by six. Even though she was not a car person and didn't know what kind of car the Maxima was there was no doubt that it was a nice car from the picture. Tracy now had a new car but it didn't come free. She was required to stay in good standard with the company and each month a small but noticeable amount would go to the charity of her choice. Tracy continued through her e-mails but it seemed like with every one she answered, she had to send a reply.

At four forty-five she decided to pick-up her car and come back to finish replying to her e-mails. After picking-up her car and parking it in her new parking spot Tracy could hardly contain herself, so she called her friend Leanna as soon as she arrived back into her office.

"Hey girl you will never guess what I just did?"

"Well it better be good because my husband is about to give me something if you know what I mean."

"Okay then I won't keep you but I just picked up my new car and parked it in my own parking spot. Now you go get your groove on while I get back to work, so I can get out of here."

"Oh my God girl I'm so proud of you. Give me a call later and we'll talk."

"Okay bye."

"Bye."

Tracy managed to read and reply to all of her e-mails before leaving the office at seven-thirty. Driving home in her new car felt like a dream come true; it was also a man magnet not that she was looking for a man but all the attention sure felt nice. When she got home she was exhausted so she ordered a pizza and went into the shower; as she was stepping out of the shower the phone rang so she pushed the speaker phone mounted in the bathroom. It was Leanna; they talked for an hour while she ate her pizza and then agreed to meet at Rick's Pub at the end of the week.

CHAPTER THREE

RACEL, VANESSA'S BABY sister, woke up extra early, so that she would be able to get to the phone company before work. She got there before the doors were even opened, so she waited outside. Once the doors opened she was the only customer in the store but she still had to wait five minutes before the same lady that opened the door came over to help her. Rachel couldn't help but think that if she was a white person she would have been served much sooner.

"Hi how may I help you?"

"I would like to change my phone number to an unlisted number please".

"Can I have your name, phone number and two pieces of ID please?" Rachel handed her the information and told her, her number. She then typed Rachel's information into her computer.

"Are you sure you want to change your number it's going to cost thirty-five dollar and I noticed that you recently had it changed about three weeks ago."

"Yes I am sure because my ex-husband keeps calling me and that's why I need you to make sure my number is unlisted." She looked at Rachel with a smirk on her face as she handed her the contract and told her to read and sign all three copies. Once they were signed Rachel handed them back, got her receipt and left.

Before heading to work she decided to stop for a coffee. Just as she was about to go inside she heard someone call out her name. She turned to look and was shocked to see Omar her first boyfriend, first love and first everything else walking towards her. It had been over four years since the last time she saw him. After she married Roger they moved out of town. Now here he was looking even finer than the last time she saw him. With one shift movement he came over to her and wrapped his arms around her as he whispered how much he missed her.

Embraced in his arms she felt warm and secure while she remembered How wonderful life used to be with him. They had dated for six year until he had to go take care of his dying mother in Jamaica. For the first two months the relationship was still strong because they keep in contact daily but it was becoming costly, so they both decided to e-mail each other. However, that didn't last very long because neither had the time to write each other, so within four months they had decided that it would be best that he contact her once he returned home. Omar was only supposed to be gone for six months then his sister would come to take care of their mother, so he could return to his life. However his sister was unable to and he stayed in Jamaica for two years before his mother died. Although they both thought about each other they knew that their relationship had come to an end because of the distance between them.

"Girl, how are you doing? It's been years since I've laid eyes on you." he said.

"I've been fine and you?" He stood back to get a better look at her while putting his finger in his mouth.

"Well girl I can see how fine you look, you not still married to that jerk of a husband are you?"

"Yes but were separated and I'm just waiting for the divorce to go through."

"That's the best news I've heard all morning. So can I have your number?" Rachel searched through her purse for the paper with her new number and wrote it on the back of her business card.

"I'll call you tonight if that's okay" he asked.

"Yes that's fine just call after seven I should be home by then if not leave a message and I'll call you back." He hugged and gave her a kiss on the cheek before walking away. Rachel stood and stared as he walked away, she then went into the donut shop ordered a large coffee and a chocolate chip muffin, before heading to work. Rachel owned Fortunate Money Financial Institution that provided financial service to her clients and members. She had over two hundred clients that hired her company to help them make wise investment; so when she arrived and saw one of her highest paying client yelling at her receptionist she quickly went over to defuse the situation.

"Hi Mr. McMillan; how are you doing this morning?"

"Ms. Phillips you are just the person I want to talk to."

"Okay Mr. McMillan let's go into my office." Once in her office she gestured for him to take a seat before she sat down behind her desk as she prayed that he wouldn't close his account with her.

"Would you like something to drink Mr. McMillan?"

"No thank you we need to talk about the representative you sent over last month to handle my account. Now I have never had any problems with anyone you have sent but this young lady has become a distraction. Her behaviour in the office it totally inappropriate; never mind the clothes she wears. My office consists of mostly men and when someone like that comes in and is flirting and carrying on like she is at a singles bar it disrupts the quality and service my company is trying to provide. Rumor has it that she has already slept with two of my employees; his wife came into the office yesterday and caused a scene when I was dealing with a client.

Rachel listened in shock as she found it hard to believe that it was Cassandra Webber, Mr. McMillan was talking about. Although she did dress very revealing at times; it also helped her to bring in a lot of male clients; so Rachel had no complaints until now. She was drawn out of her thoughts by Mr. McMillan voice asking her what she was going to do about the situation.

"I'm sorry Mr. McMillan I will remove her from your account immediately."

"That will not be enough; I don't want to work with a company that knowingly has employees like that. If she isn't terminated immediately my company no longer wishes to do business with you Ms. Phillips." With that said Mr. McMillan got up and stormed out of her office before she was able to say a word. Rachel picked up her phone and dialed her receptionist Cindy.

"Get Cassandra in my office now!"

"I'm sorry Ms. Phillips she went downstairs to pick up her new business cards. She should have been back already did you want me to call her?"

"Yes! I want her in my office as soon as possible." As much as Rachel liked Cassandra and her work was always outstanding there was no way she was going to lose Mr. McMillan's account because of her foolish ways. Twenty minutes later Cassandra knocked on her door.

"Come in." By the look on Cassandra's face Rachel knew that she had to fire her.

"Please sit down Cassandra we need to talk about the account we have with Mr. McMillan. He was in my office this morning and he was not happy with the situation that happened yesterday. Now I hate to have to do this but I'm going to have let you go. You have been with me for almost a year now and you know that I do not tolerate this kind of behaviour."

Rachel took pride in her company and wasn't going to let Cassandra take What she had worked so hard for by losing the biggest account she had. Cassandra Tried to defend her actions but Rachel didn't allow her to but she did give her a very good recommendation letter and a severance pay that would hold her for at least four months. She then called Frank the security guard to escort Cassandra out of the building. Right after she hung up the phone it rang and it was Omar asking to take her to lunch.

"Yes, that's just what I need to get out of my office."

"How about I pick you up in twenty minutes?"

"Okay that sounds fine; I'll meet you in front of the building."

Rachel then contacted the accounting department and told them that Cassandra Webber no longer worked with the company and then told Cindy to write a recommendation letter for Cassandra and to have it on her desk by the end of the day.

When Rachel arrived downstairs Omar was waiting for her; he suggested That they just walk to Red Lobster which was just around the corner. Once there Rachel ordered a rum and coke to unwind from the crazy morning she had, while Omar ordered a beer. After ordering appetizers Omar talked about old times and How much time he wasted on relationships with women he didn't love nearly as much as he loved her. They continued to talk throughout their meal and since she was in the middle of a divorce they both decided that it would be best to take it slow. After lunch Omar walked Rachel back to her office and told her he would give her a call later that night.

CHAPTER FOUR

ALTHOUGH HE DIDN'T own his own company Howard was one of the best cabinet makers at Lewis & Son Cabinetry he had been there ever since the doors opened. He was highly respected by his friends and co-workers, and he was now married to Vanessa who was a doctor at one of the finest hospitals in Toronto. Their relationship started off very rocky because Vanessa was still in medical school and Howard was paying all the bills. After knowing each other for only a year Vanessa and Howard were married in a small church with family and a few friends. Even though his father was invited he couldn't find it within himself to forgive Howard for not taking over the family business. His father refused to come to the wedding but his mother and sisters were there. Vanessa's father wanted his daughter to marry a doctor or even a lawyer but after getting to know Howard he respected and loved him like a son.

They were staying in a cockroach infested apartment while struggling to make ends meet for two years until Vanessa got pregnant. After the twins Tonya and Tianna were born they decided to move in with Vanessa's parents and ended up staying for almost two years; until the unfortunate death of her parents. They were killed in a car accident by a drunk driver who ended up with just a few scrapes and bruises. It was a very difficult time for Vanessa and her sister Rachel; they had to clear out the house and decide what they were going to do with their parents belongings. Vanessa, Howard and the girls stayed in her parents' house for nine month before it was sold. They then bought a four bedroom house closer to where Vanessa worked. With their work schedule it took them two weeks to completely move everything into the house and settle in. Once that was done they decided to meet at Rick's Pub for dinner and drinks to celebrate their new house.

Rick's Pub was the last place Howard wanted to go, however; Vanessa had insisted that they meet there after work. As he travelled on the bus to work he couldn't help thinking about how many women he had been with, inside the back room of the Pub. He was well known to the ladies and still considered himself as a player whom most of the time didn't even remember that he was married. He had cheated on his wife several times before and after they were married but she never found out.

Vanessa had accused him many times but since she couldn't prove it he denied it by reassuring her how much he loved her and the kids. He really did love his wife as most men do but he found it hard to keep his pants on around beautiful women especially when they were always coming on to him. It wasn't his fault that he was a strikingly handsome, hard working, middle class black man who looked great for his age. With skin the color of brown sugar, a body that would make must women give it up in front of her parents and gorgeous hazel eyes that made women wet their panties whenever he stirred into theirs. He was every single woman's dream but a wife's worst nightmare.

Howard arrived fifteen minutes late for work and as he walked in Louise the receptionist informed him that Mr. Edwards his boss wanted to see him but he didn't want to go.

Mr. Edwards was a very distinguished Jamaican in his late fifty's; who feared that his younger wife Charlene might divorce him for a younger man. They had been married for eight years and had met while he was on vacation in Jamaica. She was a true Jamaican girl that his brother had introduced him to; that was only twenty-seven when they got married six months later and within two years Charlene had all her papers to fly to Canada. Although she was only looking for a plane ticket and a man that could take care of her; Mr. Edwards prayed that she would one day love him as much as he loved her. He was a recovering alcoholic that just loved to talk about all the bad things that were going on in his life. Howard dreaded the thought of having to go into his office before starting work. After a five minute wait, Mr. Edwards called him into his office.

"Howard what brings you to work so late? I've been waiting all morning to talk to you."

"I told Louise I was coming in late, I'm sorry but you were already gone yesterday when I was leaving."

"Well that's water under the bridge, Charlene walked out on me last night and now she won't even answer my calls."

Mr. Edwards felt the most comfortable with Howard; he was the first person that he hired almost ten years ago, and if it wasn't for Howard his company wouldn't be what it is today. Just as Howard thought, Mr. Edwards started to tell him about his personal life; that his wife might be leaving him for a younger man and that he was taking every piece of jewelry that he had every bought her back. He was going to put them into his safety deposit box at the bank. The man was almost in tears as he spoke. He kept him in his office for almost two hours, telling him things he didn't need or care to hear. However, it was always better doing nothing with the boss and getting paid than working his ass off. When Mr. Edwards finally finished telling Howard his life story it was lunch time, so he insisted that they have lunch together. He only wanted him to stay so that they could continue their conversation but it really wasn't a conversation considering Mr. Edwards was the only one talking. After what seemed to be a lifetime with him, lunch was finally over and he was able to get to work. Although, he was behind he managed to catch up and finish everything that needed to be done by the end of the day and left with his two best friends Leroy and Tyrone. They had been friends for over twenty years and it was Howard who got them the job at Lewis and Son Cabinetry. Leroy Anderson was the nicer one of the two he always tried to make the best of every situation, his relationship with women always ended up with him being used for his kindness and left broken hearted for expressing his love. All he ever wanted was to find a nice woman to settle down with and have kids. Tyrone on the other hand was the bad boy with an edge that the women seemed to like; as much as he loved kids he never wanted any of his own because being tied to any women was not in his future plans he was a love them and leave them type of man.

As friends they were very different but the bond between them was tight and they were very loyal to each other as well to Howard. For the past few months Tyrone and Leroy were planning to make some extra money by robbing Mr. Edwards but were not sure if they wanted to let Howard know because he and Mr. Edwards were such good friends. It was Tyrone's idea to rob Mr. Edwards and the only reason he was thinking about letting Howard in on it was because he knew Mr. Edwards like the back of his hand. However Tyrone knew that it would be hard to convince Howard to be a part of the robbery but this wasn't the right time to talk about it as they walked to the bus stop. The bus was so packed that they almost weren't able to get on; once they arrived at the bus station they went their separate ways.

Howard decided to head home first and change before going to the pub to meet his wife. His mind was consistently going back to what Dr. Peterson had told him. How could this be happening? He knew he hadn't been feeling like himself lately which had caused him to miss a few days of work, but he would never have thought that he had cancer. As much as he wanted to Howard wasn't ready to tell Vanessa that he was sick. However he knew that he had no choice but to take his medication. He was so lost within his thoughts that he almost missed his stop and he forgot to pick-up the alcohol for the house warming party at his place in a couple of days. Instead of going back, he decided to pick it up tomorrow.

When he arrived home, he walked into the kitchen and noticed the light on the answering machine flashing, so he pushed the retrieval button. You have two messages.

"This message is for Mr. and Mrs. Blackwood, just a reminder that the camp bus will be leaving at 10:00 am sharp, so please have Tonya and Tianna at the church no later than 9:45 thank you". The next message was from Vanessa asking him to bring pyjamas to Ms. Bedford the babysitter because the girls were spending the night.

Before going to Ms. Bedford's he took a shower, smoked a joint and then went to drop off the clothes. Once that was done he caught the bus to Rick's Pub. The ride was very pleasant until a beautiful young black women walked on, she sat right in front of him, and then crossed her long lustrous legs. Her beauty was overwhelming; it was impossible for him not to look at her and he wasn't the only one staring. She was also looking at him. She then uncrossed her legs and came to sit beside him. She introduced herself as Candy which gave him an instant erection before his brain could think of anything to say.

Without letting his better half take control, he told her his name and that he was married. To his surprise, she was still willing to hook up with him even though she was also married. Before getting off, she handed him a business card and told him to give her a call. As she walked off the bus, his manhood responded to her every move. He looked at the card that read 'Come to Candy's For the Sweetest Rub Down in Town'; she was a massage therapist which excited him even more.

When he got off the bus, he put the card in the back of his wallet with some other cards to hide it from Vanessa. He decided to get off the bus a few stops before his stop, so that he could walk off his erection before going into Rick's. Howard sauntered gracefully into Rick's Pub on Fifth Avenue, a place he had once frequented but hadn't been there in months. It was arduous for him to bring himself back into any bar never mind this particular one. It had almost cost him his marriage and his wife didn't even know it. After finding out about his condition he just wanted to drown the pain away with alcohol and meaningless women. For four months straight he went to Rick's Pub right after work, drinking away his pay check and sleeping with an endless amount of women.

Dr. Patterson's words repeated continuously in his head like a broken record. You have pancreatic cancer. Although those weren't his exact words they were the most important words in the sentence. He then gave him a prescription for erlotinib and told Howard he needed chemotherapy at least once a month. Instead Howard filled the prescription, changed his number and hadn't been back since. It pained him to keep his condition away from his wife but he knew that she would be too concerned and he wouldn't be able to enjoy the time he had left. He had gone to see several doctors and they all came to the same conclusion which was that he was going to die and it was just a matter of time.

For several weeks Vanessa had question him about where he was spending His time, but he made her believe that he had to work late every night. However, when he did come home he was either drunk or in the worst of moods. In reality he was cheating on her, picking up young women and taking them into to the back room of the Pub or to the cheapest motel. He even started to see Tracy again; she was the one person that didn't care about everything that was going on in his life she just wanted sex.

If it wasn't for Vanessa coming down to Pub one night after Mike called her because he was too drunk to leave by himself. Howard would certainly still be spending his pay check at Rick's. That night Vanessa found lip stick on his lips and a stain on his shirt but because he was too drunk she had to wait to confront him in the morning. The next morning she sent the girls to wake him up with a bowl of ice water. Howard was in a deep sleep with alcohol still in his system when he was rudely awoken. The freezing water brought him upright drenched from the chest up. He jumped up with blood in his eyes ready to attack only to see the twins looking at him and laughing.

"What the hell are you doing?" They both replied "but daddy mommy told us to."

As he looked beyond the kids he saw Vanessa standing in the door way and from the look on her face he knew he was in trouble but he didn't even know why because he couldn't remember how he had gotten home last night. For all he knew some women had dropped him home. Vanessa told the girl's that she needed to talk to daddy, so they should go and play in their room. As the girls walked off Howard wished they would stay to protect him from whatever was about to happen. While still deep in his thoughts as to what had happened last night Vanessa flung his shirt in his face.

"What the fuck is this on your shirt. Are you fucking cheating on me?" Before he could say a word, she began crying hysterical, so he lied.

"Babes you know how much you and the girls mean to me, I would never do anything to jeopardize what we have."

"And that's your explanation."

"It's the truth. Do you think I could be out there cheating when I have all that I need right here. I love you too much to be with anyone else but you."

"But yet you haven't explained how the fucking lipstick got on your shirt."

"It was some girls' birthday and she was walking around giving every man in the pub a kiss that wasn't with a woman. When she tried to kiss me I turned my head and she caught the corner of my mouth. As for the lipstick on my shirt, she then tried to kiss me again, I moved and when she stumbled her lips caught my shirt."

Even though that much was true there was so much more that had happened before and after the kiss; that Vanessa could never know about. He did love his wife but knowing that his time was limited how could he keep his pants on around beautiful women that were always coming on to him. Howard gestured to Vanessa to come to him and even though she was reluctant, she slowly made her way to him. This wasn't the first time she had suspected something was wrong within their marriage, but she couldn't put her finger on it.

Plus he would always reassure her by telling her that it was only her imagination. He made love to her and convinced her that their marriage was stronger than ever; however it left her wondering who he learned those new moves from. Coming out of his thoughts, Howard walked towards the bar hoping he wouldn't see anyone he knew as he approached the bartender, with a grin that didn't go unnoticed.

"Hey Mike let me a have a gin and tonic."

"Hi Howard, what up? I haven't seen you in what about a month. You working hard or hardly working?

They both laughed as Mike turned to get Howard's drink. Mike Taylor was a twenty-seven year old, up and coming football player who worked as a bartender to pay for his last year in college. With light brown eyes which he got from his mother, he liked to juggle more than one relationship at a time but he also made each women feel as if she was the only one. Mike leaned over and handed Howard his drink.

"Honestly to answer your question, I've been working hard. That's why you haven't seen me around and what have you been up to?"

"Well you know how it is; just working my ass off to make ends meet. I'm surprise you would bring your tired ass back in here after what happened the last time you where here."

"I'm meeting my wife for dinner and drinks."

"Well how is that beautiful wife of yours anyways? The last time I saw her was when she came in here to bring your drunken ass home. Actually that was the last time I saw you too."

"Oh she is fine; we just bought a new house not too far from here." Howard said. Just then Mike turned to serves another customer as he signalled Howard to hold on. Howard then walked off to look for his wife, but she hadn't arrived as yet, so he went back over to the bar.

"Well married life seems to be treating you good; how are the kids?"

"Their great, their going into senior kindergarten this year, and leaving for camp tomorrow for two weeks. So you know Vanessa and I will be fucking all over the house while their gone."

"So you and Vanessa going to be working on getting a boy while the girls are gone?"

"You know how much I want a boy to carry on my name, but I don't think she's ready; plus we haven't even settled down into our new house, never mind with our mortgage payments we can't afford another child right now."

"Yeah so you're back in the old neighbourhood; at least you can afford to move somewhere decent. I'm still living in that one bedroom shithole with visitors that I have to kick out before morning because they always want to over stay their welcome."

"What happened to Jackie, I thought you two were tight?"

"That was in the past, plus she caught me with her friend."

"What! You crazy; didn't I teach you anything? Don't you know that you should never sleep with a women sister or friend and if you do don't get caught?"

"First of all it wasn't her best friend and plus I didn't even know that they knew each other. Anyways I've been back on the prowl ever since and loving every minute of it; so if you know any single black women hook a brother up."

"Actually I might be able to help you out, because we're having a house warming next weekend? Maybe you can talk your boss into placing a order, so I can get a discount on the alcohol. You know how it is nothing for nothing, isn't that your motto."

"So that means you're going to point out all the single women."

"That's not a problem" Howard replied. Just then Tracy, Leanna and two of their friends walked in and like magnet to steel her eyes were immediately drawn to the bar; her heart nearly jumped out of her chest when she saw Howard standing there. So she told her friends to grab a table while she made her way over to the bar.

"Damn! Don't turn around right now, but there is a bunch of girls over there and one of them just happens to be Tracy."

"Not hot to trot Tracy?"

"Yep, that'll be the one and she is now heading this way."

"Shit! Do you think she saw me?" Before Mike could get a chance to answer, Howard felt her arms wrap around his neck and slowly trail down his chest. He turned to find her breast in his face.

"Hi Tracey, long time no see; how have you been?"

"I'm fine and I can see you're looking even better than the last time I saw you" She replied.

"Thanks I can see you haven't changed one bit either."

"What's that supposed to mean?"

"I just meant that you're looking just as good; why so offensive?"

"I'm sorry if you took it the wrong way but I didn't mean for it to sound like that. I've had a rough day, so why don't you buy me a drink and let's call it even."

"Now Tracy why should I buy you a drink, after all the shit you put me through?"

"Because I miss you and I know you miss me too. Plus we have a lot of catching up to do." She leaned in towards him while making sure her breast was back in his face as she whispered in his ear.

"I've been a very naughty girl and I know you would love to give me a spanking, I know you miss me and all those wild and crazy nights we use to have." As she spoke she rubbed her hand up and down his inner thigh. A warm rush raced through his body as he remembered all the wild and wonderful nights they used to have. He then felt his manhood harden between his legs and knew he had to get inside of her.

"If I do recall I wasn't the only one begging for more" he replied.

They looked at each other and laughed.

"So has your taste in alcohol changed since the last time I bought you a drink?"

"No. I'll have my usual vodka and orange juice with." Howard cut her off by saying.

"With a bit of ice and a slice of lemon not lime. I know how you like it, haven't I always been able to please you in more ways than one."

"Yes you have that's why I kept coming back for more, so are you going to give me what I've been longing for?" He signal for Mike and ordered her drink, he then told her that he would be right back. He walked off with a hard on that had to be dealt with, as he stepped outside to call his wife.

"Hi Diane, can I speak with Vanessa please."

"Oh hi Mr. Blackwood, just hold the line and I'll transfer you."

"Okay thanks Diane."

"Hi honey, I'm so sorry but I'm running late I have to deal with one last patient then I'll be leaving."

"Don't worry, take your time. I'm not even there yet, I ran into Tyrone and I was just calling to see if you had left. So, how long do you think it will take before you leave?"

"It's going to take at least an hour, so I won't be able to leave until about nine; since I won't be in tomorrow, is that okay?"

"No problem, plus I'm about twenty minutes away so, I'll just get my drink on while I wait. See you soon bye babe's."

"Okay bye honey."

Howard walked back inside with pure excitement on his face, knowing that he Had more than enough time to take Tracy into the back room and give it to her good. By the time he got back she had ordered three more drinks on his tab and was feeling pretty good. After she finished her forth drink all he could think about was taking her into the back room and putting her into all of her favourite positions. She was a damn good piece of ass and one of the best lovers he ever had. They had fooled around for years before and after his marriage but she was just a good fuck. Not at all the type of women that any man would want to settle down with; considering she only knew how to please a man in the bedroom. He called Mike over and asked him if the back room still had a couch and if he could use it, he then ordered a vodka shot and a can of coke. Mike replied yes and put the shot and coke on the bar and handed him the keys with a grin on his face. Howard slowly covered his erection not wanting Tracy to know the power she still had over him, but of course she noticed.

"I see I still have the ability to make you rise to the occasion." He looked at his watch and knew he didn't have much time to waste, so he took her by the hand and lead her to the back room. As soon as the door closed she was on her knees undoing his pants. She took every inch of his erection into her mouth as her hand moved up and down his shaft. As good as it felt he didn't have time for that; he pulled her up, spun her around and lifted her dress. Just then he remembered that he no longer walked with a condom in his wallet.

"Please tell me you have a condom" he asked.

"No, but just put it in." There was no going back now he had to have her, so he entered her without any protection. He forcefully put ever inch of his harden manhood inside, then he pounded her from behind like a piece of meat that needed to be tenderized, while holding onto her hair. She moaned which aroused him but he wasn't ready to come yet, so he pulled out and told her to get on the couch. While on her back Tracy reached up to kiss him but he turned his head instead.

"No kissing just fucking because I only kiss my wife." As she laid there she felt hurt by his words but she knew this was the only way she could ever have him and for tonight it was good enough. He didn't care if he was hurting her because it was all about what he wanted as he continued fucking her. He then opened her legs as far as they would go so that he could go deeper with every stroke. Howard felt every inch of his body exploded as he released his entire load inside of her.

Tracy wanted him to re-enter her but instead he grabbed the back of her head and rammed his still hard manhood as far as it would go in her mouth. He noticed that she wasn't gagging like she used to, as he fucked her face and then released in her mouth.

"It looks like someone has mastered the art of deep throat" he said. Unable to speak she shook her head and smiled. He tasted so good as she swallowed and wiped off her mouth. Fucking her meant nothing to him but it sure felt damn good to be inside her again. There was no love making just straight fucking but something beautiful was conceived that night. He got up and buckled his pants, then left the room without saying a word to her, leaving her to compose herself before returning to her friends.

The only thing that was on Howard's mind was getting rid of Tracy before Vanessa arrived, he was so lost in his thought that he didn't notice when she emerge from the back room.

"So when can we hook up again?"

"To be honest that's the last time that will ever happen."

"Why because your married? Like that's ever stopped you before." Before he could reply, Tracy's friends came up behind her.

"Hey Tracy it's about that time; the girls are ready to go."

"Okay I'm coming." She turned to Howard. "Well it looks like I'll be leaving, but here's my number give me a call and we'll talk."

"I might just do that, it was nice seeing you again, bye." She reached down and gave him a kiss on the cheek, then walked off. It didn't even bother her that she didn't have anything to eat because having Howard inside of her was good enough and she was ready to go home.

Howard was relieved as he watched Tracy and her friends leave the pub. Just then Mike came towards him with a big grin on his face.

"So that's what married man do, when their wives are not around. I take it she doesn't know you're married?"

"Actually she knows that I'm married but that's just the type of women she is, since she can't find a man to settle down with she is willing to take whatever she can get. Howard ordered another gin and tonic, while Mike went back to work. Fifteen minutes later Vanessa walked into Rick's Pub. She walked right over to the bar where her husband was sitting. She leaned over and gave him a kiss on the lips; he responded just the way she liked by putting his tongue in her mouth.

"You want to grab a booth and I'll order some drinks" Howard asked.

"Sure, I'll have rum and coke instead of wine tonight."

"I see you want to get drunk tonight. Does that mean I can take advantage of you when we get home?"

"You can have anything you want since we will be home alone." He took her into his arms before she could walk away and whispered "I can't wait to get you home my love."

"Your dirty little mind is always at work isn't it? I hope it's not working when I'm not around."

Vanessa tried not to be a jealous woman when it came to her husband but it was hard because of all the bull shit he had put her through. She only hoped that after almost six years and two kids that he had finally gotten his act together. She walked off to find a booth near the back where there were hardly any lights. Shortly after Howard came holding a tray with: a bottle of rum, pitcher of coke and two glasses with ice.

"Oh don't tell me your moonlighting now as a bartender; don't I give you enough work to do at home?"

"Yes you do. I'm just helping Mike out he's backed up with orders." He wiggled his way into the booth beside her and poured them both a drink. He knew what he had just done with Tracy was wrong but he felt no remorse because he had no feelings for her, he loved his wife. He then put his arm around her and gently squeezed her. They talked until the waiter came to take their order.

"Hi my name is Anika are you ready to order?" Howard looked at the waiter; she was beautiful but way too young for him although she had seen him with Tracy her face did not give him away.

"Yes I'll have the jerk chicken with rice and peas."

"Would you like anything to drink with that?"

"Yes can we have a pitcher of ice water please?"

"And you sir?"

"I'll have the same with plain rice and potato salad."

"Okay your dinner will be ready shortly" The waiter walked off to place their order. By the time the waiter came back with their food; the bottle was half finished and Vanessa was one drink away from being drunk. Howard on the other hand was pouring himself another drink. Once they finished their meals; they ordered strawberry cheese cake and vanilla ice cream for dessert which Howard feed to her. Teasing her with every bite so that he could lick the ice cream he left trailing down her chin off.

"It's been a long time since we've spent time together and we'll be all alone tonight so that means we can make all the noise we want. I've missed you a lot" said Vanessa.

"I miss you too and tonight we can make up for all the lost time. I'm sure glad the girls are not going to be home because I wouldn't want them to think I was killing their mother when I put it on you later. Maybe we should try something wild and crazy if you know what I mean."

"That would be nice what did you have in mind?" she replied.

"How about we get really kinky and you can do that thing I like and actually complete the job, I could even tie you up to the bed or you can even allow me to enter where no man has gone before if you know what I mean."

"Okay that sounds good but we have to stop at 'Aren't We Naughty' and do I get to tie you up too?"

"Yes but what do you need at 'Aren't We Naughty'"?

"Well if you want to go where no man has gone before; we need to go."

"Okay let's hurry up so we can get the hell out of here then." The both laughed knowing what was going to take place once they arrived home. They finished their desert, paid and said good night to Mike before leaving. Howard looked at his wife with pure excitement in his eyes, while walking to the car.

Vanessa was so drunk she could hardly walk. She leaned against him for support as she got into the car. They drove the short distance to 'Aren't We Naughty' and because Vanessa was so drunk Howard asked her what she wanted and just went in by himself to get it; alone with some other stuff that he wanted for himself. He then pulled into the corner store without Vanessa even knowing that they had stopped and ran in picked up some wipe cream, a movie and a bottle of coke while Vanessa laid passed out in the car. Vanessa couldn't remember getting in or out of the car never mind how he had managed to get all of her clothes off. Thank God she was with her husband she thought to herself as she rolled over to Howard's side of the bed. Just then Howard walked into the room with nothing but his boxers on and holding the can of whip cream. His manhood stood fully erect which lifted his boxers up like a tent. Vanessa couldn't help but laugh as she pointed down at his hard on and he began to laugh too.

"Oh so you're laughing at the whopper (which was her nick name for his manhood) now are you?"

"No! But you look so cute. It's just waiting for me isn't it?" Howard put the movie into the VCR then danced his way over to the bed with the whip cream and bag from 'Aren't We Naughty'. With one swift movement he took off his boxers and leaped onto the bed beside her while almost hitting her with the can of whip cream. She reached over for the can but he pulled his hand away.

"Hey it was my idea to use the whip cream not yours." "If that's how you want it; it's fine with me. Did you get the anal ease because there is no way you're going to go where no man has gone without it?"

"Yes and I also got something so you can enjoy the taste when I release in your mouth."

"Oh it's nice to know you really want me to complete the job but are you sure I'm going to enjoy the taste?"

"Well I did get your favorite flavor cherry and I'm going to use it first with the whip cream." He shook the can and opened it.

"I want you to keep your eyes closed and put your hands above your head."

He then reached over and got her stocking from off the floor where he had placed them and tied her hands onto the bed post. He sprayed whip cream alone with the cherry liquid on various parts of her body and slowly licked it off. The night seemed to be endless as he put the whip cream in places he had never gone before with his tongue. He then untied her and allowed her to tie his hands. Vanessa explored his body and devoured the whopper in her mouth as she put the whip cream all over his body. Just before he exploded in her mouth she poured the liquid into her mouth and then picked up where she had left off. Within seconds she was swallowing Howard's love juice. She looked at him with a smile and said.

"Now that's a taste I could get used to."

was overwhelmed with pleaser; his whole body felt weak as he looked into Vanessa's eyes he could see the love she had for him. She untied him, put the anal ease on, positioned herself and waited for him to enter where no man has gone before. With anticipation Howard slowly entered his wife from behind while keeping in mind that this was her first time and it would be painful for her. Vanessa felt like a tree trunk was going up her ass as she fought the urge to tell him to stop; however once he was completely inside of her she was able relax and enjoy. It was an enjoyable experience but it wasn't something she wanted to do regularly. She was glad that she finally found out what the big deal was all about because all she wanted now; was for her husband to put his manhood where it really belonged. Howard's whole body trembled as he fell flat onto the bed after releasing his full load inside of her.

After more foreplay Howard was fully erect and was ready for round two. Vanessa then straddled him and rode her husband as if her life depended on it and she loved every moment of him being inside of her. He then flipped her over and entered her treasure box from behind and gave it to her hard. That night was different from all the other nights and it made Vanessa wonder who he had learned those moves from but she refused to think that he was cheating on her and went to sleep instead. The night ended with quite an explosion as they conceived their third child but little did Howard know; he got Tracey pregnant that night too.

The next morning Howard woke up and made breakfast, not out of guilt but he was hungry and he didn't think it was right to wake up his wife just to make him breakfast. While in the kitchen he called Ms. Bedford to say bye to the kids before they left for camp. Ms. Bedford was a close friend of Vanessa's parents before they passed and had spent many holidays with the Richardson family. She was now in her late sixty and has been taking care of Tonya and Tianna for almost a year. Vanessa and her sister Rachel had always like Ms. Bedford, although she was strict they loved going over to her house to play with her kids.

"Good morning Ms. Bedford".

"Boy how many times I have to tell you to call me Agatha."

"Yes sorry, it's just a respect thing Agatha. So are my girls driving you crazy?"

"You know them girl love me too much to get out of line with me".

"That's right they know you'll put them in their place if they do."

"Well my kids, your wife and her sister all grow up with my rules and they are all doing great things and now these two will do the same".

"Amen to that. Well Agatha can I speak with them please."

"Hold on let me get them." Girls your daddy is on the phone. He could hear the excitement as they rushed to get the phone. Ms. Bedford put the phone on speaker to avoid them from fighting to speak with him first. They both tried to speak at the same time telling him different stories, so Ms. Bedford told them to talk one at a time. Tonya spoke first telling him her story then allowed her sister to speak. He then brought the phone in the room so Vanessa could speak with them.

After breakfast they spent the day in bed enjoying each other's company physically, emotionally and sexually but Howard still could not find it within himself to tell her he had cancer.

CHAPTER FIVE

AFTER WEEKS OF trying to convince his wife to take some time off from work so that they could get away for a week Vanessa finally agreed. Howard made all the traveling arrangements and Ms. Bedford agreed to watch the kids while Rachel would bring and pick them up from school. Howard arranged for them to stay at an all inclusive beach resort in Jamaica. It was a couple's only resort with nineteen other couples; that had entertainment, daily tours, water activities and each room faced the beach. When they arrived Vanessa was exhausted because she went from work right to the airport and wasn't able to sleep on the plane with all the noise. After booking into the room Vanessa barely had the strength to take her shoe off before falling asleep.

While his wife slept Howard wrote her a note telling her that he would be at the bar before going downstairs for a drink. When he passed by her; his scent was overwhelming. She watched and observed him before she approached because she knew he had everything that her body ached for in a man. As he sat at the bar drinking his third vodka martini a very strikingly attractive woman sat down on the stool next to him. She introduced herself and told him that her and her husband came to this resort at least twice a year and enjoyed meeting other couples. Even though she said she was married her eyes were piercing into him and he felt like she was undressing him as she spoke; however he was glad when her husband showed up. They sat at the bar talking for awhile until Vanessa came; they then grabbed a table and ordered more drinks. When Howard introduced his wife to the couple he could see that there was a powerful and instant connection between Jerry and his wife. Vanessa's eyes lit up when she saw the six foot five handsome man standing in front of her. When he took her hand and brought it to his lips she felt an electrical shock rush through her body and she knew that she was sexually aroused by this man. At first when Howard noticed the connection he felt jealous but there was no doubt in his mind that Jerry was also attracted to his wife. However he did wondered if Jerry would allow him to be with his wife if he could convince Vanessa to agree to be with him. They spent the night getting to know each other and then at midnight they went back to their rooms. Once back in their room Howard couldn't help thinking how nice it would be to get into Samantha's pants and as he made love to his wife it was Samantha that he was thinking about.

For the next two days the four of them were almost inseparable and Vanessa even admitted that she did find Jerry attractive after Howard told her that he thought Samantha was a very alluring woman. Howard then asked Vanessa if she would allow him to sleep with Samantha if he allowed her to sleep with Jerry and surprisingly she said yes. However she never thought that he was serious when he asked the question otherwise she would have said no. The following day Howard and Vanessa spent a lovely day with Howard's family; afterwards they ate dinner with their new friends. As the night went on they all seemed to be getting alone very well while they watched the live entertainment and then they went dancing at a nearby night club. They danced the night away as they danced provocatively with each other's partner and all eyes were on them. Jerry's wife was a very flirtatious woman and Howard enjoyed every minute of her wondering hands. By the time they left the club the sun was up; Vanessa and Samantha agreed to meet for brunch and then have a spa day since they had been spending all their time with their husbands.

After taking a shower and getting ready to meet Samantha for brunch Vanessa was surprised when Howard started to complain about her going to the spa because she would be gone for three hours. However little did she know it wasn't because she was going to the spa but Howard knew that giving the opportunity to be alone with Jerry he would ask him about what was on his mind? Once the ladies were gone the two men decided to enjoy some of the water activities that the resort offered and then went to the bar for a drink. Several drinks after Howard finally had the courage to ask Jerry the big question.

"There is something I've wanted to ask you and I hope that it doesn't offend you."

"Wow! It wouldn't be that my wife wants to fuck you and I would love to fuck your wife."

Howard nearly choked on his vodka martini because he never thought it would be something they were thinking about too. The two men sat at the bar and discussed what the guidelines would be and all Howard could think about was what he was going to say to convince Vanessa but also how he would feel if she agreed.

Two hours later Vanessa walked into their hotel room feeling invigorated and relaxed as she lied on the bed next to her husband.

"How was your massage?"

"Oh my God honey that man worked every muscle in my body. It was the best massage I've ever had."

"What you mean it's even better than the ones I give you?"

"Honey you know I love your massages but come on you know that the only reasons I do is because it comes with perks".

"So what you only like my massages because of the perks?"

"Yes."

"Oh so since you've had your massage I can just give you the perks then? I'm sure your limbs are nice and limber." Before she could protest Howard pounced on her like a lion on its prey. Placing butterfly kisses as he made his way down to her treasure box and tasted her forbidden fruit. He was intoxicated by her sweet nectar as she moaned with delight he pleasured her with his tongue; he then positioned himself so that she could reciprocate. Several positions and orgasms later Vanessa was tired and sore as she got up to take a shower.

"Babes there something I want to ask you?" Vanessa pivoted on her heel and looked at her husband.

"Remember when you said that you would love to have a threesome?"

"Yes why?"

"Well I was talking to Jerry about it.?

"What! Why would you talk to a stranger about that?"

"I've seen the way you look at him and he has been watching you too. Honey I can understand if it's something that you don't want to do; I just thought I would ask."

"So why didn't you talk to me about it first?"

"I did I asked you if you would allow me to sleep with Samantha if you could sleep with Jerry and you said yes".

"Honey I never took you serious I just thought you were just joking."

"Well isn't it something you said that you have always wanted to do?"

"Yes but."

"But nothing babes this is a once in a life time opportunity so why not do it. It doesn't mean that I love you less because I want to be pleasured by two women especially when I know it's something that you have fantasized about too."

"So; Samantha has agreed to do this as well."

"Yes she has and they have both talked about this before I even mentioned it to him."

Reluctantly Vanessa agreed and went into the bathroom to take a shower. While his wife was in the shower Howard called Jerry's room and told him that they should meet in the lobby. After telling Vanessa that he was going down to the lobby; Howard met with Jerry and between the two men they booked adjoining rooms. They then went to the gift shop picked out something sexy for the other ones wife to wear. Afterwards they went upstairs to prepare the room for their ménage à trios with a CD player, candles and they left the door to the adjoining room open. Once back in his room Vanessa was in bed watching TV.

"Where did you go?"

"I went to talk to Jerry and everything is set up for tonight; so that I can make your fantasy come true."

"What!" Vanessa jolted out of bed so fast that Howard thought she was about to attack him. I can't believe you did that; are you sure this is something you want us to do?"

"Yes and I know that deep down it's something that you've also want to do; so stop thinking so much about it and let's just do it babes."

"Are you 100% sure you want us to do this because once it's done it's too late to go back" Vanessa said.

"Oh, I'm sure I want it but will you be okay with another woman sucking my cock?"

"Well will you be okay with another man fucking your pussy?"

"No but it will still be my pussy when he is done and you will never see him again".

"So what you're saying is that you're completely comfortable with me being with Jerry?"

"I can't say that I'm completely comfortable but it is a fantasy that we've both have thought about and like I said it's a once in a life time chance. With two people that we will never see again" replied Howard.

"So are they coming to our room or were going to theirs?"

"Actually we reserved an adjoining room so if at any time you don't feel comfortable I'll be there for you."

"Okay so are you doing this because you really want to be with Samantha or because you want to have a threesome?"

Howard wasn't sure how to answer that question because telling her that he really wanted to fuck Samantha might just piss her off. Instead he said that it was just a fantasy and if she wasn't comfortable with it they didn't have to go through with it. With much deliberation they sat talking about the pros and the cons. Two hours later Vanessa was putting on the pink and black crotchless, breast exposed outfit that Jerry picked out for her while her husband watched with a hard on. Without saying another word he walked over to his wife bent her over and gave it to her from behind and then said now let's go babes. When they entered the room the light in the other room was on and Vanessa heart raced with excitement, anticipation and fear but deep in her heart she knew that this was something she longed for and that's why she felt like a kid in a candy store about to get everything she wanted.

"Are you two ready in there we've been waiting? Jerry shouted.

"Yes we are. Howard replied as he kissed his wife with his fingers crossed and asked her if she was sure she wanted to go through with it and was grateful when she said yes.

"Ok babes there is a bag on the bed filled with toys, a blindfold and handcuffs whatever you want to use is up to you; remember your in charge and I'm in the next room if you need me. Howard kissed his wife and walked into the next room while Vanessa looked through the bag on the bed she then put on the blindfold and lay on the bed. Few minutes later, her legs were being spread apart and she could feel the sweet sensation of her Jerry's full lips devouring her pussy while his right hand massaged her breast. It was hard not to think about what her husband was doing in the other room but having the blindfold on made her feel like she was in a different world and it was her husband pleasuring her instead of a stranger. She could hear Samantha moaning from the other room and as much as she wanted to ignore it she couldn't so she told Jerry to put some music on. Jerry had to go into the other room to turn it on and as soon as Howard saw him he assumed something was wrong and stopped what he was doing.

"Is she okay what's going on?"

"Yes she is fine; I'm just putting some music on."

"Okay let me just talk to her for a minute." When Howard walked into the next room and saw that his wife was blindfolded he bent over and put one then two fingers inside of her as he whispered in her ear.

"Baby it's me are you sure you are okay with this?"

"Yes."

"Okay Jerry is going to come back now and baby I love you."

"I know you do and I love you too."

Seconds later Jerry was back and resumed his position between her legs but this time he had ice in his mouth. Jerry slowly pushed the ice cube into her treasure box with his tongue. While Vanessa moaned with ecstasy he continued to use his tongue as the key to her box. He then took her hand and placed it on his manhood; not being able to see she was shock to feel how thick he was. While Jerry worked his magic with his tongue; her breast were being aggressively sucked on and she knew her husband was now in the room. She then felt Jerry's thick rod was entering her awaiting pussy. Vanessa felt like she was about to explode, her body squirmed, vibrated and was just completely out of control as she lost count of how many times she came. She didn't want them to stop, her pussy lips were swollen, her breast tingle from the sensation of having them played with the whole time she was being fucked and it felt great. Howard then removed the blindfold and she noticed that Jerry was no longer in the room.

"Babes are you okay?"

"Wow baby that was quite the experience; my body is still amazed at how good it all felt and I don't feel guilty because the whole time it was you I was thinking about. However it's something I would never do again."

"Well I'm glad that you enjoyed it but it's my turn now."

"Wait you're not going to want me and Samantha to do anything because that's not part of my fantasy."

"No babes I want to eat your pussy while Samantha's sucking my dick and then you can watch me fuck her like I just watched Jerry fuck you." Samantha was an expert as she took the full length of Howard's manhood into her mouth and skillfully played with his balls at the same time. The noises that were coming from Samantha's mouth were so animated it drove Howard mad and the more Samantha enjoyed her husband the more the experience turned Vanessa on. As she watched Samantha pleasuring her husband Vanessa was so aroused that before she realized, she was playing with herself. Jerry then came back into the room and positioned Vanessa so that she could watch her husband as he gave it to her from behind. The couple went at it for hours; changing positions and partners. When it all ended Samantha and Jerry went back into their room while Vanessa fell asleep in Howard's arms.

The next morning Howard and Vanessa returned to their room and Jerry and Samantha checked out of the hotel but before leaving Jerry left a CD along with a note at the front desk for them. When the front desk called to inform them that there was a package waiting they both wondered what it could be. Howard got dressed and went downstairs to pick it up; as the lady at the front desk handed him the package she had an 'I know what you did last night' look on her face which made Howard feel very uncomfortable. Once back in the room he opened the package took out the CD and handed it to Vanessa as she was walking out of the bathroom naked while he read the note.

Hi Vanessa and Howard,

We hope that you both enjoyed your experience last night because we both did. As Samantha mentioned to Howard we come to this hotel at least twice a year and you would be amazed at how many couples there are like yourselves that want to try something new by having a threesome with someone that they don't know and will never see again; unless they want to see us again that is. Although you guys were unaware that you were being taped please be reassured that there is only one copy and it will not be posted on the internet. I suggest that if you would like to keep the video that you download passwordkeeper onto your computer. It is a program that I designed for the privacy of the couples that experience sinfulfantasies so that their CD won't get into the wrong hands; the website is www.passwordkeeper.com and also log onto our website www.sinfulfantasies.com to set up your CD. Once you have logged onto the website the password is simply me then follow the steps on how to download and save the CD onto your computer. At the end of the video we have also verbally given our word that this video will not be posted on the internet. It was very nice meeting the two of you and as I mention we enjoyed spending time with both of you.

Sincerely Jerry and Samantha

Vanessa put the CD inside the DVD player, grabbed the remote, pushed play and got back into bed. The first person she saw was herself on the bed with the blindfold on and her legs spread wide open. As Vanessa watched the video, she was aroused and she couldn't help her wandering hands as she played with her breast. Seeing herself in action was almost a bigger turn on than the actual act itself.

For the last two days they visited with more of Howard's family, watched the video and made love. Although they had traveled many times before, this was the best trip that they ever had; the experience was one that Howard knew he would never have a chance to do again. Because of his condition this would most likely be the last trip he would be able to enjoy. With their bags packed they both went down for a well needed massage before heading to the airport.

When they arrived home Vanessa unpacked their suitcases and then sat down at the computer. When she logged onto the website she was surprised to see how many followers they had and there were hundreds of stories posted from couples around the world. After reading a few stories she entered the password that Jerry gave them and a screen popped up.

To save your CD onto the computer you will need to answer three related and one non related question about your sinfulfantasies experience. After four wrong attempts to answer the questions, this video will automatically be destroyed. Once the CD is downloaded and set up onto your computer these are the questions that you will need to answer every time you watch your video.

1. *What was adjoined?*
2. *What were the colors picked out for your experience?*
3. *What two objects were used to enhance your experience?*
4. *Choose a question non related to your experience.*

When Vanessa was answering the questions Howard came into the room and sat next to her; room, pink and black, ice and blindfold and threesome.

"What are you doing?"

"Downloading the CD, so that we can destroy it before it gets into the wrong hands."

"Why did you enter in those words?"

"Those were the answers to the questions I had to answer, so that we can watch the video. Can you believe that Jerry and Samantha have been doing this for years; you should read some of the stories from other couples. It almost makes me want to have another experience but like you said it's a once in a life time opportunity Vanessa said."

"Exactly we have both fulfilled our fantasy of having a threesome and as much fun as it was I don't need to do it again."

"I totally agree with you babes. Now let's watch it again before we go to bed."

"Okay but I was thinking that we should make a video and save it on sinfulfantasies too."

CHAPTER SIX

OMAR COULDN'T STOP thinking about how wonderful it was to see Rachel again. That day they met by the phone company had confirmed his feelings for her. After his mother passed Omar moved back home and bought a three bedroom, two and a half bathroom townhouse. He was an internet supplier and was able to continue his work while in Jamaica. Omar had met and dated many beautiful women while he was in Jamaica but it was Rachel that was always on his mind. The love he felt for her never went away. He was glad that Rachel and his sister had kept in contact because whenever he asked about her his sister Kate could always tell him how she was doing. It wasn't by chance that Omar had run into Rachel that day it was because his sister told him where she worked and he was actually on his way to see her.

Omar wasted no time getting back into Rachel's life; once he found out that her good for nothing soon to be ex-husband was on his way out. However, he didn't want to force his way back but yet he couldn't stay away. He needed her to know that he was nothing like Roger; she was the only women he had ever truly loved and there was no way he was going to take the chance of losing her again.

As much as he wanted to make love to her, he knew he needed to wait until She was ready, he also knew that it would be worth the wait. For the next two weeks he wined and dined her and spent many nights cuddling on his or her sofa watching movies. He knew that her divorce would be final any day now and by then Rachel would know just how serious he was about spending the rest of his life with her.

He wanted her to be his wife and the mother of his kids, he also wanted to share everything with her and eventually he would. Omar made a conscious decision to remove all his booty calls from his cell phone, there was no need for those types of women because he only wanted Rachel.

Omar had just finished cooking dinner for one when Rachel called and asked him if he wanted to come over for dinner.

"Actually I cooked so how about you bring what you made and come over; I know you must have some Tupperware."

"Okay that sounds great; let me just jump in the shower and I'll be right over."

"See you soon babes".

Rachel took a shower, put on a very sexy wrap dress and went into the kitchen to put the food into containers; just as she was about to put her shoes on the phone rang.

"Hello."

"Hi Rachel its Cindy; Roger was in the office insisting that he talk to you. I called security and they removed him from the building and I told them that under no circumstances should he be let back into the building again. However Rachel when he was leaving he did threaten you and me and I'm very worried."

All the excitement of going over to Omar's was drained from her body as she listened to Cindy. Although it was only a matter of days before her devoice was final; Roger still could not come to terms with the fact that she wanted nothing to do with him and Rachel knew that Cindy had every right to be worried because he was a very violent man. There were too many times she had gone to work with glasses on because he had punched her and Cindy was the one person in the office that she had confided in.

Roger was the only man that ever hit her; not even her father had laid a hand on her. It was always her mother that had spanked Vanessa and her. Just thinking about her parents made her realize how much she missed them and there would be no amount of time that would make her forget how wonderful they were.

"Rachel! Are you there?"

"Yes Cindy I'm sorry. I really don't know what I'm going to have to do to get that man out of my life. However when you're leaving please make sure one of the security guards walks you to your car to be safe; also don't drive your usual way home just in case he is following you and call me as soon as you get home please."

"Okay I will bye.

"Bye."

When Rachel hung up the phone her hands were shaking with fear. Roger was making it really hard for her to move on with her life even after everything he had put her through. She decided that the first thing in the morning she was going to do was file a restraining order against him. With that decision made she put her shoes on and headed out the door. Twenty minutes later she was knocking on Omar's door. When he opened the door she almost dropped everything in her hands.

"Damn Omar are you trying to give me a heart attack?"

"Come on babes don't act like you have never seen me without my shirt on before."

"Yes I have but you didn't have all those muscles and a six pack."

"Oh does that mean you like my new look; I've been going to the gym. So are you going to stand outside all night or are you coming in?" As she walked passed him Rachel gave Omar the bag with the food.

"Does it make you feel uncomfortable being around me when I don't have a shirt on because I can put one on?"

"No I'm sure I'll be able to handle it. Now let's eat because I'm starving and you know how I get when I'm hungry".

Rachel cooked steak, potatoes and made a salad; while Omar made fried chicken with rice and peas and mix vegetables; with a fine bottle of wine they ate dinner by candle light. After dinner Omar set the mood by turning on some music and asking Rachel to dance. They danced the night way to reggae, R &B and old school jams until Omar's mixed CD was finished. He then played 'I wish you didn't love me so good' by Shirley Brown which was the song they danced to on their first date.

"This song brings back so many memories" Rachel said.

"I know it has been my favorite song ever since that night. I now have it as my ring tone whenever you call." Taking her by the hand he pulled her up into his arms and hit the replay button on the remote. It didn't take long before their dancing become very sexual and by the end of the song Omar wanted to rip her clothes off and make love to her. However, he didn't want to pressure her into doing something she may not be ready to do considering she wasn't divorced yet. Rachel never cheated on Roger when they were together; however they had been separated for almost a year and her divorce would be final in a matter of days. So when she reached down and unzipped Omar' pants she did not feel guilty for wanting him deep inside her.

Omar didn't need any more signals to let him know that he had the go ahead to have his way with her as he started to remove her top. Within seconds their clothes were scattered around the room as they made their way to the bedroom. He was thankful that he had showered before she came by. He was overwhelmed with pleasure when she took all of his manhood into her mouth.

He felt paralyzed by her mouth techniques and was amazed that she managed to get all of him inside her mouth but he wanted to taste her before he exploded. They made love until both their bodies could handle any more and fell asleep in each other's arms.

The next day when Rachel was leaving Omar's house the first thing she noticed as she got into her car was Roger's car parked across the street so she head right for the police department to file the restraining order against him.

CHAPTER SEVEN

TWO WEEKS LATER Leroy and Tyrone went over to Howard's place to watch the football game. When they walked in the kids ran down the stairs to greet them at the front door, they jumped all over Howard while almost knocking him to the ground. He bent down, kissed both of them on the cheek, and then gave Vanessa a kiss on the lips as she walked into the front hallway. Vanessa then noticed that he wasn't alone.

"Hi Leroy Hi Tyrone, how are you guys doing? They both replied then gave her a hug and a kiss; after kissing Vanessa Leroy went over to say hi to the girls while reaching into his pocket.

"Look what I have" said Leroy as he stretched out his hand and gave them both a toy. Leroy had always wanted to have kids but never found a woman he thought was worthy enough to have his child. The two men then walked into the living room.

Vanessa told the kids to say good night and brought them upstairs to get ready for bed. After they were bathed Vanessa read them a bed time story and tucked them both in, she then went back downstairs into the kitchen to get Howard his dinner.

"Leroy! Tyrone! You guys want something to eat?" Knowing that they wouldn't refuse her food she took three plates down from the cupboard. Howard got up and went into the kitchen, sneaking up behind his wife and grabbing her ass as he kissed her on her neck. Vanessa nearly jumping out of her skin as she put the plates down and turned around. She then wrapped her arms around him.

"How was work, babes? He asked.

"It was stressful. I have some paperwork to do but I did get a promotion and I'm getting my own office babes."

"That's great honey. Does that mean we have something to celebrate tonight?"

"We sure do babes I'll just finish my paperwork and then I'm going to take a long bath and head to bed; so don't keep me waiting because I might just fall asleep."

He then kissed her, while almost sticking his tongue down her throat. Tyrone then yelled out, "What's going on with the food?." Before she could answer he released her and went back into the living room. As he walked in Leroy said.

"You're one lucky man; I need to find me someone as fine as your wife."

"Yeah you do need to find someone and keep your eyes off my wife. Don't you have a girlfriend how come I haven't heard you talking about her lately, Mandy isn't that her name?"

"Don't even mention that bitch's name I broke up with her about a month ago. She's into women" responded Leroy.

"She's what!" Tyrone said.

"You heard me right; she even wanted me to join in that night I caught her and her girlfriend naked in our bed kissing."

"Don't tell me you turned that opportunity down, you know how many men would love to have a chance like that? Two women at once doing each other and that want to do you too. Now that's what I'm talking about. Oh my God, I'd have to be out of my fucking mind before I would say no to that," said Tyrone.

In the kitchen, Vanessa put Leroy and Tyrone's dinner on a tray and brought it out to the living room. As she entered the room, she could hear the tail end of the conversation loud and clear. Howard then jumped in on the conversation by saying.

"I would take that offer in a blink of any eye."

Not noticing that his wife had entered the room, he continued to tell his boys how much he would enjoy being with two women if he weren't married. Vanessa cleared her throat and said. "Is that so honey? I'm glad were married". With a serious look on her face she then said

"I hope that means that I have nothing to worry about?" He laughed as he watched her bend over to put the tray down. He then looked up at his friends to see if they were watching her too, but they weren't. Just then the phone rang and Vanessa went back into the kitchen to answer it.

"Hello."

"Hey girl how are you doing?"

"I'm fine. So when are you going to come see us; since you are just around the corner now?" said Vanessa.

"Actually I've been waiting for my invitation".

"Oh so when do you need an invitation to come to my house, all those other times you were knocking on my door without an invite and now you need one. The kids have been asking me when you are coming to see their new room".

"I will come over before the house warming party".

"I really hope so because I miss you a lot you're all the family I have left besides Howard and the kids. Can you hold on for a one minute please?"

"Sure; I'll just run to the bathroom" Rachel said. Vanessa placed the phone on the table and put Howard's dinner on a tray before bringing it out to him. She then went back into the kitchen and picked up the phone.

"Hello! Hello! Are you still there Rachel?"

"I'm here".

"So how is everything at work going? Vanessa asked.

"I've been really busy at work because I now have to find someone to replace Cassandra. I hardly have time to myself plus Omar has been keeping me very busy too" Rachel said.

"What! Why would you need to find someone to replace Cassandra and when did you start talking to Omar again? Vanessa asked.

"I almost lost my biggest client because she was sleeping with two guys from the company and one was married. Mr. McMillan came to my office and insisted that I let her go or he would cancel his account with me; so I had no choice but to fire her."

"Wow that's messed up and now tell me how long have you been talking to Omar?"

"Well I bumped into him when I was leaving the phone company two weeks ago and we have been seeing each other every day since".

"Damn has it been that long since we've talked. So have you done the nasty with him yet?"

"Well actually we have I just couldn't fight it any longer but I do feel guilty because I'm not a single woman yet."

"Although you and Roger are still married you have been separated long enough. So there is no reason for you to feel guilty."

"You're right considering I have no intention of ever getting back with him and I am ready to move on with my life."

"Well I'll be so happy when that day comes because I never did like Roger and Omar has always been the true love of your life."

"I know and spending time with him again almost feels like we were never apart."

"Oh by the way did you invite Lorraine and Kim to the party?"

"Of course, I invite the girls. They are both coming. Oh and did you hear about Lorraine's new boyfriend; he's only twenty-six said Rachel."

"What! She is thirty-seven. What the hell is she doing with someone so young?"

"I know and when I mentioned it to her she went off on me saying he has his own place and got money in his pocket."

"So what if he has money he's probably a drug dealer. You know this is an all-time low for her, what she can't find a man her age?" Vanessa asked.

"That's exactly what I asked her and she said it's not a matter of the age she's looking for someone that's going to treat her the way she deserves to be treated and apparently this little kid does. Well we'll all get to meet him she has invited him to the party" replied Rachel.

"Well I can't wait to meet this youngster that is servicing our friend" Vanessa said.

"Oh yeah before I forget to tell you she wants us to go out with Kim and her for New Year's Eve. It would be Kim, Richard, Lorraine and her youngster, you and Howard, Omar and me" said Rachel.

"Where are they going?"

"Either to Q10 or Rocket it's the two hottest clubs downtown, plus it's the only place we could fine that has dinner and dancing on New Year's Eve."

"What type of crowd is it because I don't want to be spending the night with a bunch of youngsters like Lorraine's boy toy?"

"Oh hell no; both clubs are for grown folks".

"Okay I'll ask Howard if we're doing anything that night but girl I have to go do some paperwork; I'll talk to you tomorrow. I love you bye."

"Love you too bye." Grateful that the girls were finally asleep Vanessa went into her office to finish her paperwork before going into the shower.

After they finished eating Howard brought their plates into the kitchen and washed the dishes. Just as he was about to leave the kitchen, Leroy who was smoking a cigarette and rolling a joint, yelled out for him to bring an ashtray. Howard turned, grabbed one off the counter and went back into the living room. He placed it on the table, picked up a beer and sat down. Leroy put out his cigarette and lit his joint, took a pull then blew the smoke in Tyrone's direction. Tyrone who had been tuned into the football game, turned toward Leroy.

"Give me some of that. As he reached over, took the joint and inhaled three times then tried to pass it to Howard but he was half asleep. Leroy nudged Howard as he took the joint from Tyrone.

"Hey man why you always so tired? You got a night job we don't know about Leroy asked?"

"He's probably cheating on his wife again and doing both women is too much work for him to handle" Tyrone said.

"Lower your God damn voice before my wife hears you and at least I got a real women mother fucker" Howard laughed.

"Okay so why have you been so drained lately?"

"Well we're not the only ones who have noticed because Mr. Edwards has been watching you and asking questions too" said Leroy. Howard sat up in his chair, with a clued outlook on his face. Then he replied.

"That fat fucker even shortened my paycheck, he said how I'm slacking off on the job and he'll put the money back once he sees some changes. He had the nerves to say how it looks like I'm losing weight and that my wife must not be feeding me right. I just looked at him because I knew that the words that I wanted to say to him would get me fired. Vanessa also thinks something must be up, she want me to go to the doctor's tomorrow. She even made an appointment and everything" said Howard.

"I think you should go; besides if there is something wrong don't you want to know. I would want to know if something was wrong with me plus Vanessa and all of us including Mr. Edwards are just looking out for your best interest, so go and see what's up" Leroy said.

Although Howard already knew what that problem was he wasn't ready to tell anyone why he was always so tired.

"I already know what's wrong; I'm just not ready to tell her or anyone what it is yet."

"Well if you know what the problem is what are you going to do about it?" asked Tyrone.

"Don't worry about it I'm dealing with it in my own way."

"Listen, Howard, Leroy and I have a plan to make some money, you want in on it or what? Tyrone said because he wanted to change the subject."

"How much trouble will it get my ass into?" asked Howard.

"Well the way I figure is if it's done right none but it's between the three of us, it doesn't leave this room is that clear?"

"I hear you so go on tell me what's the plan."

"Okay check this out, we're going to rob old man Edward's."

"What! Your fucking joking right because you guys must be out of your minds."

"This isn't a joke; did you know that every Saturday night he brings the weekly cash to the bank? Just think about it he always uses the back entrance of the bank because it's closed at that time of the night. Plus it's dark and there is less traffic back there. If we position ourselves right, it will go down smoothly" said Tyrone.

"The only thing is he always has someone with him and he always carries a gun" said Leroy.

"You two have this shit all figured out right. What the hell we going to do if they pull their guns on us; say were sorry and run?" asked Howard. They both laughed then Tyrone said. "Your ass can but I'll be pulling my piece out on them."

"So not only do you want to rob him but you will be carrying a gun too and just where are we going to get a gun from?" Howard said.

"Well if we need guns my cousin from New York can get us some without any problems" said Leroy.

"Okay what we will do is wait until next week when Mr. Edwards has that big sell out sale. So Leroy, will you be able to get the guns by then?"

"I'll get on it tomorrow, I don't see why he wouldn't be able to get them for us by mid-week" he replied.

Just then Howard heard Vanessa's walking around upstairs and told his friends to lower their voices. Vanessa was oblivious to what was going on down stairs as she went into the bathroom to take a shower. She turned on the shower, slipped out of her clothes and stepped into the shower. She was about to wash her hair but decided against it because she would have to blow dry it too. She picked up the soap and wash cloth, lathered herself while brushing the rag across her breast, she felt the sweet tingling sensation rush throughout her body as she moaned and was instantly aroused. She continued to playing with herself as she wished it was her husband's strong hands touching her instead of her own. While thinking about Howard, she realized that they were going to have their own night of hot passionate love making as soon as his friends were gone. So she decided it would be worth it to wait for her husband to satisfy her.

Fifteen minutes later she dried herself off and slipped under the sheets naked to wait for her husband. Howard could hear Vanessa getting out of the bathroom and wanted to get up there as soon as possible. He stretched his arms in the air and yawned; trying to hint that he wanted to get to bed.

"Now this is what we'll do; you and I will grab them from behind while Leroy gets the money bag. We'll only use the guns if we absolutely have to, plus we'll be positioned before they even get there" Tyrone said.

"The only thing I don't like is that we'll be using guns otherwise it's a good plan" said Howard.

"I don't give a damn about what you think, but while I'm covering your ass, I would feel much safer knowing that you're able to cover mine. However, if you're not cut out for the job just say it and Leroy and I will do it ourselves. Just as long as you keep your mouth shut" replied Tyrone.

"Well I'll have to think about it, but I will let you know by tomorrow if I'm in or not because I'm going to bed now" said Howard.

"Yeah you do just that, I'll talk to my cousin about getting us the guns and we'll talk in the morning" Leroy said. They both got up, said good-byes and left; Howard then locked the door behind them, cleaned up the living room and went upstairs. He slowly tip-toed into the room, took off his clothes and prayed she wasn't sleeping yet.

From the instant Vanessa heard Howard coming up the stairs she became excited, she laid still and waited for him. With one quick gesture, he slid under the covers wrapped his arms around her waist, and then he moved his hands towards her breast and squeezed gently. Vanessa tried to contain herself but she couldn't it was always hard to resist him. She let out a soft sexual moan as she felt the hardness of his manhood press against her. There was a big grin on his face as she turned around to face him; she then placed her hand on the whopper. Like a wild animal he devoured her as he forced every inch of his manhood inside of her. She opened up with sweet anticipation as she allowed him to go deep within her. Howard's excitement didn't last for too long because within minutes it was over but she didn't care because no matter how quickly he ejaculated he always satisfied her, plus she knew she could pick up where he left off in the morning. She moved closer to him, nuzzled in his arms and went to sleep.

Howard on the other hand couldn't sleep he laid starring at the ceiling, thinking about what Tyrone and Leroy was going to do. Under normal circumstances he would have never even considered doing anything like that but with his condition getting worse he felt he had nothing to lose.

The next morning Vanessa was running late, so she reminded Howard about his doctor's appointment and was out the door before he could even give her a kiss good bye.

Reluctantly Howard went to his appointment although he had already missed four since finding out about his condition and if it wasn't for his wife he wouldn't even be here now. He arrived just on time and was glad to see that no one else was waiting as the last patient walked out of the doctor's office. Dr. Patterson who had been Howard's doctor for fifteen years was one of the few white people he trusted.

Howard could tell that Dr. Patterson was going to nail into him about missing his appointments as he summoned for him to come into his office.

"Mr. Blackwood (Which is what he called him when he was upset with him) it's been four months and four missed appointments since I've seen you last, now I've explained your situation to you and you know how important it is for you to take your medication. I know the last time we spoke I told you that you may have up to two years to live but if you're not taking your medication there is less of a chance that you will even live that long. So how have you been feeling?"

"Well my wife feels that I need a check-up."

"Have you been feeling any different lately?"

"Yes I've been sleeping a lot, I've lost weight and I can't seem to hold any food down."

"So you have told your wife?"

"No she just thinks I'm coming down with something."

"Howard your wife is a doctor it's only a matter of time before she will see that something is wrong and it's very important that you let your family know."

"I will soon."

"Well I strongly believe that if you have chemotherapy treatments and take your medication you will live longer. What I need you to do is take off your clothes, so I can give you a full check-up and I'll be right back."

At that moment Howard knew why he hadn't visited the doctor more often; it was because he hated getting undressed for a man. The doctor came back into the room and gave Howard a full physical, blood test and then handed him a urine bottle.

"Fill this up and return it to the front desk" said Dr. Patterson. Howard returned with a full bottle and handed it to the receptionist, then went back into the office. After waiting for over an hour Dr. Patterson walked in with the results. From the look on his face Howard knew that it wasn't good news. The doctor sat on the edge of his desk (which was something he never did) and told Howard that because he wasn't taking his medication his condition had gotten worse. Howard listened to every word Dr. Patterson had to say but couldn't believe what he was hearing. How could this be happening? At that point he knew exactly what he had to do which was rob Mr. Edward so that Vanessa could take care of the girls once he was gone. Howard stood lifelessly, and walked towards the door; his whole body trembled with every step he took. Dr. Patterson called to him and he stopped.

"Now Howard it's very important that you take your medication, here is your prescription. I could be wrong about how much time you have left but I really think it's time you tell your family and friends." said Dr. Patterson as he gave Howard his prescription.

"Will this make me live any longer?" he said as he took the prescription from the doctor and walked right passed the receptionist as if she wasn't even there and left the office. He walked outside and caught the 63D bus to work while thinking to himself that this day could not get any fucking worse.

At work he didn't say much he just wanted the day to be over so he could go home to his wife. He didn't talk to anyone unless they asked him a question, not even Tyrone or Leroy he just did his work and went right home at the end of the day. Instead of taking the bus he took a cab home, so that he could have some alone time before Vanessa got home.

When he arrived home he went right into the shower and cried his heart out like a baby for more reason than one. First of all he was dying and leaving his family behind and secondly he was about to do something that he would never do under normal circumstance but he wanted his family to be okay financially once he was gone. There were so many things in his life that he still wanted to do; like take the kids to Disney World, watch his girls grow up, buy another car, have a vacation home in Jamaica and so much more but now he would never be able to do any of them things. Dr. Patterson's word kept ringing in his head.

"I could be wrong about how much time you have left but I really think it's time you tell your family and friends" he said as he gave Howard his prescription. Even if he was wrong about how much time he had left he was still going to die it was just a matter of how much time he had left and no one but God knew that answer. While he was getting out of the shower he could hear Vanessa yelling at the girls about putting their shoes away. He quickly put on a pair of track pants and went downstairs.

"Hi honey how was your day?"

"It was fine until I picked up the girls; they have been fighting all the way home and they are getting on my last nerve".

"Daddy Tianna said I like Sheldon just because I gave him my snack but I don't he's just my friend" said Tonya.

"Yes you do because you always sit beside him and not me."

"Okay girls, that is enough; now Tianna if your sister says their only friends that's all they are plus you both are too young to have a boyfriend anyways." Okay daddy Tonya said but Howard could see that it wasn't the end of it for Tianna however she knew better to say another word about it in front of her parents.

"How would you girls like to go out for dinner after you finish your homework?"

Both girls were excited while Vanessa looked on amazed at how Howard always knew how to defuse a situation with the kids. After they were done their homework Howard took the girls to Captain Jack's Burger Joint while Vanessa stayed home and did paperwork. As Howard watched his girls eat; his heart ached knowing that he wouldn't be able to see them grow up. There was so much he was going to miss out on; their lives had just started. He would never get to go to their graduations, watch them go out on their first dates; see them develop into young ladies. It wasn't until Tianna asked why he was crying that he even realized that he could taste his tears. Lost for word he told her that he was just so happy to have such wonderful girls and how much he loved them. Once they were done the girls went and played in the play area as Howard watched with a few other parents.

CHAPTER EIGHT

RACHEL WAS JUST about to jump into the shower when the phone rang.

"Hello"

"Good morning is Mrs. Lancaster there please?"

"Yes, this is her but I know longer go by that name, I'd rather you call me Ms. Phillips, how may I help you?"

"This is sergeant McCall we have Roger Lancaster here in custody. He was found drunk and wondering around without any shoe or coat on. When we brought him into the station he assaulted the officer and has been placed under arrest. We then realized that Mr. Lancaster was in possession of a quarter pound of cocaine. The officer refused to remove his handcuffs because of his behavior to make a call and has asked that we call you to arrange bail.

"By the way how did you get my number?"

"Mr. Lancaster gave it to me so I could call you."

"I'm not sure how he got my number because it's unlisted but Mr. Lancaster and I will soon be divorce and I don't wish to help him; so he'll have to contact someone else."

"Bye Sergeant McCall."

"Wait Ms. Phillips he wants to talk with you." Before she could protest she heard Roger's voice on the other line.

"Hi baby, how you doing? I've been missing you, I know that it's been awhile since we've talked but I really need your help. I really don't know who else to turn to."

"Look Roger I don't know how you got my number but that's beside the point! I told you once and I'll tell you again I don't want to have anything to do with you.

The divorce will be final in a few days and that is the only time I will have to deal with you again, so you'll just have to call someone else to bail your sorry ass out. Bye!"

"Rachel wait do not hang up on me please." His plea for help went unheard because all he could hear was the dial tone.

"That bitch! I can't believe she hung up on me, she'll pay for that mark my words she'll pay dearly as soon as I get out of here!" He didn't realized how loud he was talking until officer McCall asked him if he was making threats.

"No officer, I'm just frustrated."

As Roger was being taken back to his cell he couldn't help but to think how much he still loved Rachel and although he knew she would never give him another chance; he wanted her to pay for turning her back on him. He was going to protest the divorce but with these charges and him not being able to go to court in a few days there was no way he could do anything about it behind bars. He knew that with these charges plus he was already on probation for his previous charges; that he was looking at least ten to fifteen years.

After Rachel hung up she just stood there unable to move. She wondered how the hell Roger had gotten her number; it was only two weeks since she had changed her number. Although she knew that Roger was only allowed one phone call she kept the phone off the hook She went into the shower even though she was in no mood to go to work but she had to because there were six possible candidates, she had to interview to replace Cassandra. Knowing that she wouldn't be able to go to the phone company before work; once she arrived at work she checked her schedule to see if she could go at lunch but she was completely booked until four.

Just then Cindy called her to let her know that her first appointment was here; so she told her not to schedule any appointments after four because she would be leaving early. By the fourth interview Rachel knew who she wanted to hire but still had to interview the other two. She was an older woman that had worked for one of the top accounting firms in the States until her husband was offered an engineering job at Pearson International Airport. Once Rachel was done interviewing all six candidates, she was returning her e-mails when her phone rang.

"Hello"

"Hi Rachel; how have you been?"

"Hi sis I'm fine."

"Are you sure; you sound stressed."

"Well to be honest Roger called me this morning from jail."

"What! Didn't you just get your number change the other day?"

"Yes and that's what worries me. I'm going down to the phone company after work and have it changed again."

"You better let them know that you are not paying to have it changed again because if it's restricted how the hell did he get your number."

"Enough about me, I forgot to ask you the other night how was your trip?" Rachel asked.

"Oh my God girl it was great but if I tell you how great I'm going to have to kill you."

"It was that good?"

"Yes and maybe one day I will tell you about it but I'm still savouring the moment."

"Well I can't wait until that day comes."

"Okay on a different note are you still coming by early on Saturday to help me with the party right? Vanessa asked."

"Of course what time do you want me to come by?"

"Around six would be good. Are Kim and Lorraine coming too?"

"Yeah their coming; I've taken the day off tomorrow and the three of us are having a late lunch do you want to join us?

"No I won't be able to I have a meetings all day".

"Well I'll see you on Saturday I have to get back to work."

"Okay bye I love you."

"I love you too Rachel" replied.

The conversation with her sister took much longer than she thought but thankfully she was still able to catch the phone company before it closed. When she arrived there were six customers in front of her and she was the last person they allowed through the doors. After a twenty minute wait she was finally able to change her number again without having to pay. she then noticed one of Roger's friends standing in the back.

"Is that Tyrell back there?" she asked the lady.

"Yes, would you like me to get him for you?"

"Yes please."

Without having to say a word Rachel knew that it was Tyrell who gave her number to Roger, his face couldn't conceal his guilt. Although she had always liked Tyrell she didn't want to take the chance of him doing it again; so she told him that if Roger ever got her number again, even if he wasn't the person that gave it to him she would make sure he got fired. She then drove home and was glad that she didn't have to go back to the office.

Once she arrived home she was exhausted, so she cleaned the kitchen, took a shower and laid down. As she laid naked across her king size bed Rachel's mind was in turmoil as tired as she was her body ached to be touched sexually. It had been so long since Rachel had any contact with a man that just the thought of how nice it was being with Omar the other night made her want more. When Rachel was dating Omar years ago they were constantly fucking and just thinking about him aroused her.

The thought of him inside of her made her moist between the legs; so she pleasured herself until she fell asleep. At eleven o'clock Omar called and woke her up complaining that he couldn't sleep because she was on his mind. They talked for an hour before Rachel told him that she was too tired to stay on the phone and she would talk to him tomorrow. Reluctantly Omar ended the call and decided to read 'The Power of the Subconscious Mind' before falling asleep.

The next morning Rachel was glad she didn't have to go to work; after going for a jog to clear her head she made a light breakfast and went back to bed. However, thoughts of Roger hurting her kept her awake; so she decided to go shopping to buy something for Vanessa's new house before meeting up with the girls for lunch.

She was able to get four wall paintings and a few things for the girl's before she realized it was time to leave to meet for lunch at Teaze a very upscale lounge that Rachel had always wanted to go to but never found the time. When she arrived Lorraine and Kim were already there waiting at the bar; while making her way over a lady bumped into her.

"Oh I'm sorry."

"Marsha Teasdale is that you?"

"Oh my God Rachel it's been years since I've seen you and I just saw Kim and Lorraine by the bar."

"Yeah I'm here to meet them. So how have you been doing?"

"I've been great I've been married to Ronald McMillan for fifteen years, with four kids and this is my place."

"You own Teaze? Oh did you name it Teaze because you have always been a tease or because of your last name?"

They both started to laugh because Marsha was the biggest tease and biggest liar back in high school. She left a lot of guys with blue balls and a lot of girls waiting to kick her ass. However Rachel was shocked to find out that she was married to Ronald because Lorraine's sister had been dating him for the past eight years. Although they didn't have any kids together Ronald treated Kim's sisters kids like they were his own.

"Actually it's because of both." Marsha said. "So what have you been doing with yourself?"

"Well I own Fortunate Money Financial Institute, my divorce will be final on Monday and I have no kids."

"Wow I never knew you owned that company my father-in-law is one of your clients."

"Oh what's his name?"

"Jeffery McMillan."

Through the corner of her eyes Rachel could see Lorraine giving her a not so pleasant look; so she gave Marsha her business card and told her to give her a call. They hugged and she made her way over to the bar.

"Sorry to keep you guys waiting but you know how Marsha is when she starts to talk about herself; it's hard to shut her up."

"It's okay; let's get a table because I'm hungry" said Lorraine.

Lorraine had nothing against Marsha personally it just made her skin boil when she saw her because it always reminded Lorraine of how naïve her sister was for being with a married man. Her sister had devoted her life to a man that was married and had no intentions of leaving his wife. Although Ronald treated her sister very good by taking care of her bills, bring her on weekend trip and he spent three nights a week with her and the kids he still wasn't the right man for her sister. Pushing those thoughts to the back of her mind. Lorraine ordered a lobster in a creamy butter sauce, potatoes and steam vegetables; after she realized that Rachel and Kim were waiting for her to place her order. They enjoyed appetizers and wine while waiting for their lunch.

Almost three hours later they paid the bill and agree that Rachel would pick them up tomorrow for Vanessa's party. While driving home Rachel called Omar and told him to meet her at her place and Steveroy came to pick up Lorraine and brought her back to his place. Kim on the other hand walked the short distance home; although Rachel had offered to give her a drive she decided to just walk. On her way home she called Richard.

"Hi babes what's up?"

"Nothing I'm still at the office doing paper work. How was lunch with the girls?"

"It was nice but I have an appetite for something else."

"Oh is that so. Is my baby still hungry?"

"Yes she is and what are you going to do about it?"

"Well I can't leave the office but how about you come here and I will satisfy your hunger. Be ready in half an hour my driver will come by and pick you up."

With that said Richard hung up the phone. Kim started to walk faster so that she could get home and get ready. Richard Saunders was a family lawyer at Famo Law Firm and was working on his biggest case; he was also living off of a trust fund left by his grandmother. Although he was a married man his marriage had been over for three years; the only reason he stayed was because of his son. It was hard at times but Kim did believe Richard when he told her that he no longer slept in the same bed as his wife because many nights they would be on the phone and he never would lower his voice when he spoke. He never complained when she called or when she sent him dirty text messages; as well he slept at her place at least three sometime four nights a week. So in Kim's mind she was in a relationship with a man that didn't live with her but spent many nights in her bed.

After asking his driver to pick-up Kim, Richard saved his work onto the computer and took a shower in his private bathroom. Kim was ready and waiting when the driver pulled up; instead of going right to his office she asked the driver to stop at the drugstore to pick up some condoms. When she arrived Richard was lying on his leather couch naked with his very hard manhood standing at attention. As she walked towards him he told her to stop and take off her clothes because he wanted her naked by the time she got to him. Without hesitation Kim did as she was told and was standing completely naked by the time she reached the couch.

"Now Mrs. James you mentioned that you were hungry and I have a sausage here that has your name all over it."

"Wow Mr. Saunders that is a very big sausage are you sure that's all for me?"

"Oh baby like I said it's got your name on it and all I want to do it fill your mouth and that sweet pussy of yours with my sausage." Kim drop to her knees and devoured his sausage while positioning herself, so that Richard could reach her sweetness and play with her while she pleasured him.

An hour later they were in the shower and as they continued to pleasure each other Richard told her that he loved her; although he didn't mean for the words to slip out it was the truth. The more time he spent with Kim the more he knew that it was time to end his marriage and move on with his life. Considering his son was suffering the most because his marriage had become very violent and toxic. His wife had turned into a real bitch and all she wanted was his money. His words shocked her as she swallowed but she couldn't help thinking that he only said he loved her because she had just allowed him to release his entire load in her mouth. Once home Kim was exhausted and was very glad that she showered in Richard's office before she left because she had just enough strength to take off her clothes and slip into bed.

CHAPTER NINE

HOWARD AND VANESSA were lying in each other's arms until they were rudely interrupted by Leroy's phone call.

"Hi Vanessa, can I speak with Howard please?"

"Hi Leroy hold on a second."

As she handed Howard the phone she tried to get out of bed but he held onto her waist.

"You're not going anywhere."

"What!" Leroy asked.

"Hold on." Still holding onto his wife he whispered in her ear that he wasn't finish with her yet.

"What's up?"

"Tyrone wants us to meet at his house to go over everything in an hour."

"Okay I'll be there." They hung up and Howard returned his attention back to his wife.

"Listen babes I'm going to head over to Tyrone's, so how about we take a shower, make love once more and you get everything ready for tonight while I'm gone."

"I thought we were going to do this together and now you're going to Tyrone's."

"Yeah I know but I need to deal with some stuff. Plus didn't you say your sister, Kim and Lorraine will be coming over early to help you. I really don't want to be here with you and your girls. I'm sure you all have things to talk about that you don't want me to hear."

"Well you got me there. However, the sooner we get into the shower the sooner you'll be on your way." Without hesitation Howard followed her into the bathroom. As they stepped into the shower, Vanessa slowly moved her hands across his chest and there was no doubt in Howard's mind that his wife loved him. He wanted to stay with her forever but his forever was almost over, so he enjoyed every inch of her body while he made love to her.

Afterwards, Howard took a cab to Tyrone's and on his way there he kept thinking about what he was about to do; he was still having second thoughts. However, he knew that if their plans of robbing Mr. Edwards went smoothly, he would be able to rest in peace. The thought of not being able to see his girls grow up sent shivers down his spine, but he knew it was something that was going to happen. It was only a matter of time before Vanessa and the kids would have to find out about his condition. As much as he wanted to keep it a secret from them, he was beginning to lose weight and had abdominal pain.

The medication that Dr. Patterson had prescribed for him was the only thing he was taking and he thought it was time he considered chemotherapy. So, he made up his mind that he was going to make an appointment with Dr. Patterson and take Vanessa with him and have Dr. Patterson explain everything to her. Considering Vanessa was a doctor he was amazed that he was still able to keep it from her for almost six months. However, he only kept it from her because he didn't know how she was going to handle it when she did find out.

Howard was so lost in his thoughts that when the cab pulled up in front of Tyrone's apartment building he didn't even realized; until he heard the cab driver yelling at him. Pushing his thoughts to the back of his mind, so that he could completely concentrate on what was about to take place in less than six hours he paid the drive and got out of the cab.

Throughout his whole life Howard had managed to keep himself out of jail, and never once was he involved in any criminal act. Now he was willing to risk everything to secure his family's future. He entered the building, buzzed up, and Leroy opened the door for him. When he knocked on the front door, Leroy yelled out for him to come in; he went in and locked the door behind him. After taking his shoes off, he went into the living room to see both men with guns in their hands. It took Howard aback as he took a deep breath and walked towards them. Tyrone's apartment was small but it looked even smaller because he kept it very messy. As Howard walked in, he glanced around for somewhere to sit. Everywhere he looked there was garbage or clothes, so, finally, he just shoved a pile of clothes aside and sat down.

"Where is your gun? I really hope you didn't forget to bring it."

"Don't worry about it; it's in my pocket," replied Howard.

"It better be because you might need it tonight" Tyrone said.

"You two better not start up because we all have to stick together on this" said Leroy.

Leroy could feel the tension between the two of them, ever since the guns were brought into the plan. He knew Howard was not keened on using a gun, especially because he and Mr. Edward were somewhat friends. He felt caught in the middle because he could understand both sides. He wasn't thrilled about having to use a gun, but it would be nice to know that if he did need it, it was available.

"Give it to me. Let me put the bullets in or did you want to do it?" asked Tyrone.

Howard took the gun out and handed it to him. By the way he held the gun; Tyrone and Leroy both could see that he was still not comfortable with having to use it. After putting the bullets in, Tyrone handed it back to him.

"Let's just go over everything one more time and get the fuck out of here" said Howard.

As usual, Tyrone took over the conversation. He told Leroy that his job was to get the bag out of Mr. Edwards's hand; Howard would grab the body guard and he'd grab Mr. Edwards. He then went on to tell them that the most important thing to remember is that they didn't have much time, that they couldn't let anyone see them and they needed the money bag. Once we grab Mr. Edward and his body guard, it's up to you, Leroy, to get the bag.

As soon as he's got the bag, we knock them out and run. We can't waste any time; it's that simple. He then threw a ski mask and gloves in each of their directions.

"Before we leave we have to cover the car in some way just in case someone sees us, so what we'll do is tape something over the plates. Now, is there anything that you two want to add, or could we just get the fuck out of here?" said Tyrone. They both decided not to say anything. With his ski mask and gloves in hand Howard tucked his gun into the back waist of his pants, as the three men left Tyrone's place without saying a word. It was a good thing Leroy was able to get his mother's car because otherwise it would be hard to rob Mr. Edwards in a cab or on feet. As they took the elevator Howard felt sick to his stomach and as soon as they stepped outside, he threw up in the bushes.

"If you can't stomach what we are about to do you can always back out?"

"Don't worry about me I'll be fine."

"Okay then let's do this." They got into Leroy's mom's car and drove off in the direction of the bank; with Howard in the back feeling like he could throw up again.

CHAPTER TEN

RACHEL PICKED UP Kim and Lorraine before heading over to her sisters. As Vanessa opened the door she thought how nice it was of her sister and friends to come over early to help. There was no way she would have been able to do it all by herself especially considering Howard wasn't around. Throughout the years, he was very helpful around the house; however, lately, for some reason, he wasn't as helpful as he once was. She couldn't figure out why he seemed so, tired all the time. They came in and hugged each other and headed for the kitchen.

"So girl how about you tell us what needs to be done?" Kim asked.

"Well most of the food is cooked; the decorations need to be put up. I need to clean up the living room, kitchen, and the bathrooms and make some finger food but first let me get you ladies a drink while we catch up on each other's lives." Vanessa replied, as they all headed towards the kitchen.

"That sounds good, I'm sure Lorraine would love to tell us what she has been up to" Rachel said.

"What's that suppose to mean?" Vanessa asked although she already knew what her sister was talking about. A clueless Kim looked at Lorraine for an answer. "Well is someone going to tell me" Kim asked.

"Well now I'm going to have to tell. To make a long story short I'm seeing a twenty-seven year old name Steveroy." Lorraine said.

"What are you serious; you know he could be your son. Girl what are you thinking" Kim asked.

"First of all I'm not that old and like I told Rachel, age is nothing but a number plus you know my track record with men." Just then Vanessa cut her off by saying

"This man, you mean boy".

"No! I mean man, said Lorraine as she continued. Let me tell you all, that this man makes more money than any man I've been with, has a house and a condo, as well three cars, not to mention he takes damn good care of me. He has a three year old daughter, but there is no baby momma drama going on with him. So, really and truly I really don't care who thinks he's too young for me because for the first time in my life a man wants to put me first.

Most importantly he isn't a drug dealer he owns his own business, we have great conversation, spend lots of time together and he knows how to get down and nasty if you know what I mean. This man can put it on me like no other man has before, so like I said I really don't care who has anything to say. Oh yeah and he has even introduced me to his family and his mother loves me, his daughter adores me and I adore her so, I really don't think that I'm just a ship passing in the night for him. His mother even invited me to the family reunion in Jamaica next month. I was surprised that she asked me and not him but his mother said he told her that if she approves of me than invite me, so she did. Steveroy wants me to stay a month and he is playing for everything, so the way I look at it is that I only live once and I'm going to enjoy it to the max."

"Wow! Okay girl you don't have to convince me that I should just mind my own business and be happy for you because you seem to be glowing" Vanessa said.

"That's right and thanks I needed to hear that because I am happy, I would even go as far as saying that I may be in love with this guy but instead I'll just enjoy every day that I get to spend with him."

"Well I can't wait to meet him tonight, he seems to be a great guy and most importantly he is making you happy and that's what we all want for you because you deserve it girl" said Rachel.

"So, how about you, Rachel and Kim are you bring anyone tonight?" Lorraine asked.

By the smile on Rachel's face it was obvious that she was also bringing someone.

"Well who is it?" she asked.

"Do you remember Omar?"

"Who could forget him" Kim said.

"When did you start seeing him again? Lorraine asked.

"Couple of weeks ago and we've been seeing each other every day since".

"So, when were you going to tell us? Kim asked.

"Well to be honest I wasn't trying to hide it, it's just that we've all been so busy" replied Rachel.

Kim knew that the question was now coming to her and she only wished that the guy that she had invited was her man and not just one of her baker's dozen. It was only five months into the year and she had already slept with nine men. She had asked Richard who she had been sleeping with on and off for two years because out of all the men she had been with he was the one she wished would stay. Plus they all knew and liked him. Kim sometimes felt as if there was something wrong with her because she just couldn't get enough sex. It really didn't help that she owned her own adult phone line and talked about sex all day. Her company was doing extremely well; she had over sixty regulars that would call her at least 3-4 times a week; along with referrals and first time callers. A lot of the men she slept with were turned on when she would talk dirty to one of her clients while they were servicing her. Vanessa had known Kim for four years and she considered her as a floater, someone that never had a steady man but always talked about the men she slept with. It was just a nicer way of calling her a slut considering they were friend. Rachel brought her out of her thoughts by asking her the question.

"Richard" she replied with no other explanation.

They brought their glasses up and cheers to Lorraine's new man, Vanessa's New house, Rachel reuniting with Omar and Kim bringing Richard. Kim was surprised when Lorraine asked if she wanted to come with her and Steveroy to Jamaica but gladly accepted the offer. The four friends continued to catch up on each other's lives until the phone rang. It was Howard's friend Mike Taylor asking what time the party was starting. After telling him the time Vanessa realized that it was time they get to work before the guest arrived.

They divided what needed to be done and got to work, by eight-thirty they were all able to take a shower, get ready and relax in the living room as they waited for the guest to arrive they shared a bottle of wine.

CHAPTER ELEVEN

HOWARD, TYRONE AND Leroy took the long way to bank so that they could go over everything one more time. Before long they pulled up in front of the bank and put the car in park with the engine still running.

The three men positioned themselves outside as they watched Mr. Edwards and his bodyguard pull up at the back entrance of the bank; just as they knew they would. They got out of the car and Mr. Edwards pulled out the bag from the backseat and walked towards the bank. Just when Tyrone was about to grab Mr. Edwards he stepped on something and Mr. Edwards turned around. So instead of grabbing him from the back he took hold of him from the front. Howard grabbed the bodyguard and held him in a tight choke hold. Mr. Edwards on the other hand, struggled to free himself, but Tyrone had a tight grip on him. While struggling he managed to reach into his front pocket and pull out his gun. When Leroy realized what he was doing he tried to get to his gun but Mr. Edwards shot him in the chest. Both Howard and Tyrone yelled out in anger as Tyrone threw Mr. Edwards to the ground, knocking the gun out of his hand. He then kicked the gun away and took out his own; filled with anger he looked over at Leroy fighting for his life before shooting Mr. Edwards between his eyes. He then told Howard to let go of the bodyguard; with hesitation he finally released him. Once he was free the bodyguard began to beg for his life; as he slowly backed away. He was just about to run when Tyrone lifted his hand with the gun and fired a shot into his shoulder. He fell to the ground in pain but managed to get his phone and dial 911. Tyrone stepped on the phone just as he was about to put it to his ear, breaking it into two.

In a state of shock, Howard ran over to Leroy and bent down beside him as tears ran down his face. He then put Leroy's head on his lap and held him as he listened to his best friend struggle to fight for his life.

"You were the best friend I ever had, that's why I love you. You have always been there for me; even now in the end you're here. Howard you have a beautiful wife and wonderful kids do right by them because you are a lucky man to have them"

With tears in his eyes Leroy said bye with his last breath, before dying in Howard's arms.

Meanwhile Tyrone was suffocating the bodyguard and watching the life drain from his eyes; he then picked up the money bag and called out to Howard.

"We got to get the fuck out of here, now!" Tyrone yelled. Howard kissed Leroy on the forehead closed his eyes and placed his head back onto the ground. Everything happened so fast that he didn't even think about someone hearing the gun shots and coming out to see what was going on.

"Come on! Let's go!" Tyrone shouted. With blood all over him, Howard stood up, wiped off his gun and placed it in the bodyguard's hand. They both ran back to the car and drove off.

Not too long after, they were back at Tyrone's building and Tyrone told him to park in the back; before going into the building Howard zipped up his jacket. Once again he was back inside of Tyrone's junk yard of an apartment but this time the mess didn't faze him. He paced the apartment not caring what he was stepping on. Tyrone on the other hand cleared a spot on the floor, emptied the bag and told Howard to sit down because he was making him nervous.

"Holy shit Howard this is a lot of money!" he said.

"Is that all you can fucking think about? Leroy's dead; he's fucking dead man," replied Howard as he sat on the edge of the couch. Tyrone looked at Howard with a crazy look in his eyes, then said

"Don't you think I know that? It's my fucking fault he's dead. I was the one holding Mr. Edwards, not you. I should have stopped him, but I'll be damned if I'm not going enjoy this money. I loved him as much as you and I'll miss him but I know he would want us to enjoy this money".

Howard watched Tyrone with disgust as he continued to count the money with greed in his eyes. Tyrone acted as if he was a little kid with a bag full of candy. In the past years of knowing Tyrone, Howard knew that he could be very cold-hearted, but it wasn't until today, that he really showed how unfeeling he could be. Leroy and he were friends for years; they had gone through a lot of shit together. Now it seemed as if he didn't even know Leroy or cared about who he was.

Howard stood up and walked into the bathroom, with tears in his eyes he looked into the mirror but he didn't like what he saw. It wasn't supposed to happen this way, he began praying for forgiveness but yet he knew that he had to take his share of the money for his family. He stood looking into the mirror for about ten minutes before his arms would move and allow him to clean the blood off of himself. His body trembled with every attempt he made to clean the blood off. A part of him didn't want to clean it off because it was a part of Leroy, but he had to. Once he was done getting the blood off his jacket he took his shirt off and threw it in the garbage, washed his face and hands. He then returned into the living room to find Tyrone still amazed at all the money. While Howard was in the bathroom Tyrone kept having flashback of everything that had happened. Every time it replayed in his head there was no doubt that it was his fault Leroy was dead. He was supposed to be covering Leroy but instead he was too busy trying to get the money. When he was finish counting the money he separated it into two stacks, just then Howard emerged from the bathroom.

"Holy shit Howard, there is over $650,000.00 here plus the jewellery in the bag. Listen I'll just take 150,000.00 and the jewellery."

Knowing that he would have no use for the jewellery, he agreed. Besides, it would be awhile before Tyrone could sell them on the streets. Just then a dark cloud came over Howard's face as he remembered why he robbed Mr. Edwards. He sat quietly while Tyrone danced around the room saying, were rich over and over again. With a sudden jolt, Howard jumped up and said, "What time is it?"

"It's almost ten why."

"Oh shit! We have to go Vanessa is probably wondering what's taking me so long. Put the money away and let's go."

Tyrone shoved his half under the couch and put Howard's back into the bag. "Here's your half."

"I can't take that home right now. Vanessa is going to want to know what's in the bag; keep it here and I'll pick it up tomorrow."

They then went over everything that had happened that night and their alibi to make sure there was no evidence to link either one of them to the rubbery or the deaths. Once they were done Tyrone went into his room to change; as he walked off Howard knew that their friendship would never be the same again and it wasn't only because of the lost of their friend.

When they arrived outside of Tyrone's building instead of getting a ride. Howard decided to walk the five blocks home. While Tyrone dropped the car off at Leroy's house and took a cab to Howard's. While walking he reflected on his life with Leroy: how they had met, the good times, hard time and the straight up bad times.

At that moment Howard knew that Leroy was the best friend he would ever have. Now he had to go home; lie to his wife about where he was; where Leroy was and act like everything was normal. It's not that Howard had never lied to his wife before but now that Leroy was dead; this would be the worst lie he would ever have to tell. Leroy had always stuck by his side, even when he was cheating on his wife. There were so many times Howard told Vanessa he was with Leroy when he wasn't and if she called he would just put her on hold and then three way the call to Howard's cell like he was there with him. Even though Howard didn't always tell Leroy what he was up to, Leroy knew what to do whenever Vanessa would call because it was Leroy who always had his back and now he was gone.

CHAPTER TWELVE

VANESSA WAS PISSED off that she could not get a hold of her husband who should have been home almost two hours ago. She didn't want her guest to know that she was unable to reach him so, she smiled as she lied that he was on his way. The good thing was that the music was rocking and the house was packed with people. Rachel and Omar were in their own world as they attended bar.

While Lorraine and Kim were in the kitchen talking about old times and what was going on in each other's lives. Vanessa walked around, with a glass of rum and coke in her hand and made sure that all her guest had a drink or something to eat. After a while, she went into the kitchen to get something to eat. The alcohol was taking affect on her. When Tyrone arrived he was glad when he saw Vanessa going into the kitchen because he really didn't want her to see him before

Howard arrived. Instead of saying hi he walked over to the bar because he really needed a drink and he would rather talk to Rachel than Vanessa. As Vanessa walked into the kitchen it was obvious that she had been drinking.

"Girl, how much have you had to drink? Lorraine ask"

"Oh, I don't know. I'm sure the bartenders would be able to answer that question. Do you want me to ask them?"

"No, that will be alright but I think you need to eat something before you drink anymore."

In one big slur, loud enough for everyone to hear, she said.

"That's why I came in here and where the hell is my husband it's almost ten thirty!" Kim placed the food on the table, took her glass and gave her a drink of water; as she sat down to eat. Not long after, they could hear sirens outside and could see the flashing lights through the kitchen window. It seemed to go on for quite a while like something big was happening. Vanessa prayed for her husband's safety.

CHAPTER THIRTEEN

EVEN THOUGH, TRACY'S home pregnancy test was positive she still scheduled a doctor's appointment because she needed to hear it from a doctor that she was pregnant. It had been almost two months since she slept with Howard and yet he hadn't returned any of her calls. The last time they spoke was three weeks ago and Tracy was still having trouble believing, everything he had said to her. To this day his words kept replaying in her head like a knife in a wound it hurt more and more every day. She loved him more than any other man that she'd ever been with. After all this time she just couldn't figure out why he treated her like that. With tears in her eyes she got out of bed and went into the bathroom.

As she looked into the mirror she saw someone she didn't even recognized at all. Her eyes were red and puffy with dried up tear lines from the night before on her face. This was so unlike her to let any man get to her like this but her heart ached for Howard. Maybe it was because she was pregnant but she was feeling very emotional and felt the urge to crash Howard's party he was having tonight. Her first instinct was to have an abortion but why should her baby have to suffer for her mistakes. Although Howard didn't want to be with her; he still had a right to know that she was pregnant with his child. If Howard didn't want anything to do with their baby, then that was his lost not hers? Tracy knew that she could take care of their baby by herself but he or she would know who their father was whether he liked it or not. Tracy was raised by parents who weren't ready to be parents. Although, her parents were together there were many times when she wished that they weren't. Her father brought other women home while her mother was too drunk to do anything about it. Tracy's older brother practically raised her; he was the one that made sure she had something to eat and clothes to wear. Her parents were too caught up in their own drama to care about the child they didn't want in the first place. Her older brother was fifteen by the time she was born and having to leave her job and take care of a new born wasn't part of her mother's dreams. After giving birth to Tracy her mother gained so much weight that her father was no longer attracted to her and that led to her mother's drinking. She was the only kid on her block that didn't have a curfew; as long as she didn't wake up her parents when she came home they didn't care. She was spending her late nights with Trevor; her father's friend son. He opened her pleasure box when she was only fourteen; showing her a world of sexual pleasure. Trevor was the love of her life until he moved to the States on a basketball scholarship; they kept in touch for a year until he told her he met someone else and thought it would be best if she move on as well. It wasn't until her older brother died from Aids that she realized that she needed to get away. It was too painful watching her parents blame each for his death.

She left home the day after her fifteenth birthday after telling her parent that she only wanted money for her birthday. She had been saving up for this day and had a total of six hundred dollar when she left. When she left home she was able to stay with her new boyfriend Derrick; who was five years older than her. From the moment Tracy moved in with him her life was no longer her own. He was a big time drug dealer that also had a few girls out on the street working for him. Although he never put Tracy on the street to work; he would rent a hotel room and have his high paying clients have their way with her. Derrick liked to watch and he never allowed anyone to enter her from the front; they were only allowed to give her anal sex because her pussy belonged to him. Her first experiance with anything entering her from behind was when Derrick started to use a butt plug while pleasuring her with his tongue. Mixed with the pain there was pleasure; a pleasure she had never felt before causing her to want more and soon there was no pain just pleasure. Introducing her to the butt plug was just his away of preparing her for his clients.

Hearing her stomach rumble brought her out of her thoughts and made her realize how hungry she was. While making something to eat she decided that the best thing to do was go see Howard Monday at work and tell him that she was pregnant; instead of crashing his party. Memories of her past were very painful but now she was going to be a mother and she wasn't going to allow those memories to taint the way she raised her baby.

CHAPTER FOURTEEN

THE HOUSE WAS packed with people and at ten-thirty Howard walked in. By the look on Vanessa's face, Howard knew he was in trouble, but he passed it off like nothing was wrong. As he walked through the house, he could see and hear people; some of them were even talking to him, but his mind was only on Leroy and how he would have to pretend like everything was alright. He went into the kitchen to get something to eat, hoping it would take his mind off of Leroy but Vanessa was right behind him.

"Where the hell have you been and where's Leroy? I thought he was coming with you."

"I had some things to take care of, and I don't know where Leroy is I haven't seen him. I'm sorry I didn't call you; I got caught up in what I was doing."

"And what was that!"

"I don't want to talk about it right now. Let's just enjoy the party." He turned his back to her and opened the pot on the stove; then went into the cupboard to get a plate and a cup. He then filled his plate with food, but as he was about to walk out of the kitchen Vanessa stopped him.

"I asked you a question." In a firm but not rude voice, he told her that he didn't care to talk about it right now and walked out of the kitchen with his food in his hand. She watched him as he left the kitchen and went over to the bar for a drink. Even though he knew Rachel would start up with him about where he was he needed a drink. Without looking at Rachel he asked Omar to fix him a double shot of rum with just a little bit of coke and no ice?

"I see the host of the night has finally decided to show his face. Did you talk to your wife? She has been very worried about you."

"We will talk as soon as everyone is gone if it's any of your business." Omar handed him his drink and he walked away before Rachel could say another word. With everything that was going on in his mind he knew that he had to remain calm and act as if everything was normal. As he sat to eat his food his mind was still on Leroy. It was hard to believe he was gone and what made it even worst; is that he had to leave him lying there. The DJ was playing old school and the whole place was rocking. Everyone was dancing, having a great time; even Tyrone was up on his feet dancing with one of Vanessa's co-workers. It was hard for him to believe that Tyrone could act as if it had never happened that Leroy wasn't dead because of the money. Howard thought about the old saying that "Money is the root of all evil" and how much it was absolutely true. As well how life was so fucked up because the things you want and need are the things you're best to do without but you can't. The music kept everyone on their feet until three-thirty in the morning and by four the house was almost empty.

When Vanessa saw Rachel, Omar and some drunk guy that she didn't recognize about to leave, she realized that Howard was nowhere in sight. She kissed her sister, said good night to Omar and escorted the drunken man out of her house. After locking the door behind him, she went upstairs to find her husband fast asleep on her side of the bed. Instead of waking him, she decided to talk to him in the morning besides she was too tired to fight with him right now. She undressed and slipped under the covers beside him.

The next morning, as mad as Vanessa was, she managed to make breakfast for her husband. She brought it up to him hoping that they would be able to talk about last night while they eat. Considering they both didn't have to work and the kids had slept at Mrs. Bedford's house. When she arrived upstairs he was already awake watching television. She placed the tray on the table beside him, walked around to the other side of the bed and sat down.

"Are you alright?" she asked.

"Why wouldn't I be? Howard replied.

"So are you ready to talk about whatever was or is on your mind?"

"No, but I am sorry about last night; I had a lot on my mind and I shouldn't have taken it out on you." Just then a news flash came on about a shooting at the Canada Trust bank that caught both of their attentions. Last night, three men were shot dead after a rubbery gone bad. Found were Robert Edwards of Lewis & Son Cabinetry, his bodyguard and one of his employees. They were found dead in the back parking lot of the bank. There were no witnesses to the senseless death of the three men; however, there seemed to be at least one other individuals involved. Police are still investigating, but have no suspects at this time. Police are asking if anyone has seen or heard anything last night between the hours of 8:00 and 11:00pm to please contact 222-chat. More details to follow.

"Oh my God I can't believe Mr. Edward's is dead." Vanessa said.

"I know I'm really going to miss him; he was a better father to me than my own father was."

"I knew something big was happening last night."

"Why would you say that?" said Howard.

"Because I heard the sirens and I saw the flashing lights."

"Oh."

"Is that why you were so late last night; do you know anything about what happened?" she asked.

"How would I know anything? I was with Tyrone last night."

"Is that why Tyrone got here before you and you didn't even arrive until twenty minutes after he did?"

"I was with him he drove over here and I decided to walk what's the big deal!"

"It isn't a big deal but when you're yelling at me it makes me feel like you're not telling me everything. Is there something you want to tell me?"

"No! There is nothing I'm not telling you."

"I was just wondering that's all. Plus, where was Leroy? Wasn't he supposed to come with you?"

"I don't know. He called Tyrone and told him that he was coming by his place, so we waited for him, but he never showed up. I haven't seen or heard from him since we left work. That's why I took so long we were waiting for Leroy."

"But, why were you so rude to me just now?"

"I wasn't rude. I told you I didn't want to talk, that's all. Plus, I wasn't feeling well and I did apologize for raising my voice at you."

"So, how are you feeling now?" she asked

"Am feeling better, but tomorrow I have another doctor's appointment. I want you to come with me; it's at 12:30."

"That's not a problem, but why do you want me to come?" considering all of the other times, I didn't even know that you were even going to the doctor's?"

"I just feel that we haven't been as close as we used to be, and I miss that."

"I'm glad you came to your senses because I was starting to wonder what was up with you."

"You know I love you. Don't you?"

"Of course, I do and you know I love you too?"

"There's a lot of stuff happening in my life that you don't know about, but it's not like I don't want to tell you. It's just so hard for me to talk about it."

"You know you can talk to me about anything. So what's on your mind?"

"Are you sure you want to hear what it is?"

"Yes."

Knowing that he couldn't tell her about last night; he told her bits and pieces about his condition because he didn't want her to feel sorry for him. The only thing he didn't tell her was that he was going to die. Instead, he promised that he would be there for her and the girls. Just then, the phone rang.

"Don't answer it. Whoever it is can leave a message," said Howard.

"I have to; it might be the hospital." Even thought she didn't want to answer it, she did.

"Hello"

"Hi Vanessa, is Howard there, please?"

"Yes, but first let me ask you a question."

"Yes what is it?"

"Was Howard with you last night, waiting for Leroy at your place?"

"Yes".

"So why did you get her before he did?"

"Because he felt like walking I drove over. Why?"

"Nothing I just wanted to know that's all. Hold on." She handed him the phone and started taking off her clothes as she went into the bathroom to take a shower. Howard was glad when he saw the door closed and the shower turn on.

"Did you watch the news?" Tyrone asked.

"Yeah."

"Leroy's mother called me this morning she wants me to go with her to the police station to identify the body. I don't want to go, Howard, but how can I tell her, no. How am I going to face her? This woman has been like a mother to me ever since my mother died. I love her with all my heart, and now, because of me, she is going to feel pain." This was the first time since everything happened, Howard could hear the sympathy in Tyrone's voice, for once, he wasn't just thinking about himself. "The only thing you can do is to go with her and act as if you didn't know and comfort her like she did for you."

"I want to be there for her but how?"

"Just by being there for her and comforting her because we both know that she isn't going to like what she sees."

"Okay thanks. I got to go. I'll talk to you when I get back. Bye."

"Bye."

Howard had a million things rushing through his head but it wasn't until he heard his wife singing in the shower that he got up to join her. He quickly undressed himself and stepped into the shower. He almost gave her a heart attack since she didn't see or hear him come in because she was washing the shampoo out of her hair. Just seeing her wet, naked body got him aroused. His manhood stood at its fullest attention as he pushed it up against her lower back. Instead of turning around she bent over, braced herself and told him to put it in. They were in the shower for quite awhile, doing it in as many positions as their confined space would allow. They even turned the shower off so that they could get their groove on without getting water in their eyes. Still aroused they left the bathroom dripping wet.

Instead of getting dressed they dried off and got into bed and stayed there all day enjoying each other's nakedness. Vanessa even turned her phone off after calling the hospital and letting her assistance know that she could be paged if there was an emergency.

CHAPTER FIFTEEN

TYRONE WAS UNABLE to sleep, he kept seeing Leroy in his dreams. Leroy kept asking him why he didn't cover him. He was a nerves wreck as he pulled up to Mrs. Anderson's house, he hadn't seen Leroy's mother in months. She was waiting for him on her front porch, so he jumped out to help her into his car.

Mrs. Anderson was in her mid seventies with four kids; Leroy was her only son and her only child that didn't give her any grandkids. It was hard for Tyrone to concentrate on the road there because Mrs. Anderson just kept on talking about Leroy, how he was as a child, how hard he had worked to put himself through college and how overly protected he was when it came to his sister and herself. She went on to say that she had always admire the respect he had showed toward the women in his life, but then she started crying uncontrollably when she realized that she had spoken in past tense about her son.

As much as she didn't want to believe it Mrs. Anderson felt in her heart that it might just be her son's dead body that she would have to look at. It was so unlike Leroy not to call or answer her calls and she had been trying to reach him since yesterday. Not wanting to lie to Mrs. Anderson Tyrone placed his hand over hers and told her that no matter what happened, he would be here for you. The rest of the drive they reminded silent until Mrs. Anderson realized that they were parked in front of the hospital.

"I can't do this Tyrone what if it's him, how am I going to handle it?"

"Mrs. Anderson please remember that no matter what happens I'm here for you and you have the love and support of your family too. So let's go in there with a positive attitude." She looked over at him and forced a smile because she knew that no matter what happened in there he would feel the same joy or pain she felt.

Twenty minutes later Dr. Pinkosky and Detective Myers escorted Mrs. Anderson and Tyrone towards the morgue. As they walked Tyrone held onto her hand knowing that she would not like the outcome, Dr. Pinkosky slowly removed the sheet. From the pressure Mrs. Anderson was putting on his hand Tyrone wanted to yank his hand out of hers but he knew he couldn't. She needed his support especially after seeing that it was Leroy body lying on the table. She became hysterical, as Tyrone and Detective Myers had to drag her away from the body and get her to sign some papers.

It was amazing, that he was able to drive without crashing because Mrs. Anderson was crying at the top of her lungs and swinging her arms, like a mad woman. Ever, so often her hand would hit Tyrone causing him to swerve. Knowing that he would not be able to leave her he stopped at the drugstore, without telling her what he was doing. He ran in and picked up some over the counter sleeping pills. Once they arrived at her house; it took awhile for him to convince Mrs. Anderson to take the pills but thirty minutes later she was fast asleep.

Tyrone needed to get out of there as soon as possible; so he called her daughters, to make sure one of them could be with her once he left. Once he was sure that she would be taken care of he locked the door and put the keys under the flower pot at the side of the house. Which is where he had told Leroy's eldest sister Paulette it would be; he took two of Mrs. Anderson's sleeping pills because he knew he would need it once he got home. When he arrived home he took the pills with a shot of rum, removed his clothes, turned off the phone and got into bed, it didn't take long before he was out like a light.

CHAPTER SIXTEEN

THE NEXT MORNING the paper read, "Still No Witness to the Senseless Murder of Robert Edwards, his body guard Bill Cain and his employee Leroy Anderson." There were pictures of the three men plastered on every news channel as Howard tried to find something else to watch. He was glad that Vanessa had to leave early for work because he wasn't in the mood to answer any of the questions she would be asking him. He picked up the phone to call Tyrone, but the answering machine came on so he hung up; he then got ready for work.

When Howard arrived at work, the first person he saw was Mrs. Edwards; he walked over to her to give her his condolences, but instead, she broke down in his arms.

"Who could do such a thing to him? Why Howard? And your friend, what was he doing there? Do you know anything about that?"

"I don't know, but he was supposed to meet Tyrone and me that night and he didn't show up. I'm so sorry for your loss, Mrs. Edwards, and if there is anything I can do for you, please let me know."

"Thank you Howard. I know how much my husband admired you. Since I won't be able to take over right away, I would love for you to make sure everything is going smoothly until I can get on my feet, however, I won't be needing you until next week; so I'll call you and let you know when. Is that Okay with you?"

"Yes that would be fine." Before leaving Howard called Tyrone again, and this time he answered.

"Hey! What's up? How comes you didn't come into work today? We have to act normal, so that we don't give anyone a reason to think we had anything to do with what happened and where have you been I've been trying to call you all morning?"

"Okay one question at a time. Nothings up, I took sleeping pills last night because there was too much on my mind after I dropped Mrs. Anderson home."

"How did it go yesterday?"

"Well to be honest it was the worst thing I've ever had to do. She just about had a nervous breakdown, so I gave her some sleeping pills and called Paulette to come stay with her."

"Well I spoke with Mrs. Edwards this morning and she told me that the office will be closed for a couple of days but she wants me to run our department until she can figure out what's going to happen with the company. Are you going to be home? I thought I'd drop by because I really don't like talking on the phone about this" Howard said.

"Sure that's not a problem, you coming right now?" replied Tyrone.

"Yeah I'm just going to hang around her for a while then I'll head over in about an hour."

Howard ended up staying much longer than he had planned because Mrs. Edwards wanted him to help her call the employees and let them know there would be no work until further notice. He now knew how Tyrone felt when he had to go to the morgue with Mrs. Anderson. Having to pretend that he knew nothing about what had happened as Mrs. Edwards couldn't stop crying. Three hours later Howard was finally able to leave and he was so exhausted from having to comforting Mrs. Edwards he decided to take a cab to Tyrone's.

On Saturday Howard, Vanessa, Rachel, Omar and Tyrone all went to the funeral in Omar's Jeep. There was almost four hundred people attended Leroy's funeral. There was family from Jamaica, the States and England that travelled the distance to say their finally farewell to a man that was well loved and respected. It was hard for Howard to view Leroy's open casket, never mind say good-bye to him for the last time. Almost half of the people there went up to show their respect and love. With a lot of crying and comforting throughout the ceremony, it was a long and hard day for Howard and Tyrone. Howard who found it hard to hold back his tears was shocked to see Tyrone actually break down as they lowered the casket into the ground.

Afterwards, they went back to Leroy's mother's house to have something to eat. Due to the amount of people that showed up, Mrs. Anderson had to let most of the guest go into the back yard. Parking, on the other hand, was backed up. A lot of people had to park many blocks away from the house. Mrs. Anderson walked around with a picture of her only son held tight to her chest repeating; why did this have to happen? Leroy was such a nice person, and now he's gone. Although everybody there tried to comfort her, there wasn't anything anyone could say or do. Leroy's sister Paulette took her mother upstairs, gave her two sleeping pills and got her to lie down. The night ended with everyone gathering in the back yard to say one last final prayer to the life of Leroy Anderson.

For the next couple of weeks Mrs. Anderson stayed in bed with the family album held tight to her chest. Her life had been turned upside down and all the life was drained from her once she lost her son. Every day since he was gone was hard for her; she only got out of bed to use the bathroom and get something to eat. It wasn't until her daughter told her that Tyrone was a suspect in Leroy's death that she got the strength to leave the house.

CHAPTER SEVENTEEN

RACHEL AND OMAR spent most of the day in bed making love and watching TV and at two o'clock his pager when off. It was Anthony from the office calling; he picked up the phone and dialed the number.

"Hey Anthony what's up? You know you caught me at a bad time."

"I'm sorry but you're going to have to come into the office."

"Why"

"It's Mr. Belmont he is flying in to close the deal and I know you don't want to lose his business."

"What time does his plane land?"

"It's landing at five and there's still some paper work that needs to be done."

"Okay I'll be there by three. Have Nikki meet him at the airport. Tell her to take the long way back to the office and make sure you pull his file and have everything that needs to be signed ready for me when I get there. Is that understood?"

"Yes boss". He hung up the phone and got right to work. Omar placed the receiver on the hook and turned to Rachel.

"I guess you heard everything."

"Yes and I understand but why is it going to take almost two hour for you to get dress".

"If you can't figure it out maybe I should get dress now".

"Oh no you don't I want you to tell me why".

"Is that what you really want or should I just show you why?"

"Now that sounds even better come show me why."

Within minutes he was inside of her making love to her just the way she liked it. Afterwards they took a shower together and Omar just couldn't resist being inside her one more time before leaving. They dried each other off and she watched him get dress while she lay on the bed naked.

"You're so bad you know that" Omar said. With a devilish look on her face she replied "Yeah I know and I also know that you love it when I'm bad."

"I really wish I could stay here with you but I can't afford to lose this account. I hope you can understand that I'd rather be with you."

"I do understand; I'm just playing with you."

"Well how about you stay here and rest because you're going to need your rest for when I get back."

"How long are you going to be gone?"

"I should be back by at least eight-thirty or nine."

"Okay then I'll go over to my place and pick up some more clothes if you don't mind and grab something to eat".

"That's a good idea. Get dress, I'll drop you on my way and you can take a cab back but only if you promise to be naked when I come home."

"It's a deal."

When Rachel got home the first thing she noticed was the light flashing on her answering machine indicating that she had a message. There were both from the night before. The first one was from Vanessa asking if she was coming over; the other from Lorraine. First she called her sister but no one answered; just when she was about to call Lorraine the phone rang.

"Hi babes, I forgot to give you the keys but I told Mr. Goodman the door man to let you in. just tell him your name and he'll give you the keys. I got to go love you babes." Before she could say a word he was gone. She pushed the hang up button and dialed Lorraine's number; she picked up on the second ring.

"Hello"

"Hey girl what's up?"

"I'm about to meet Kim for an early dinner." Lorraine replied.

"Well I just came home to grab some clothes then I'm heading over to Omar's for the night".

"Oh so you two are good like that. I'm glad because he makes you happy."

"He actually does."

"I was going to ask you if you wanted to come with us to that new Chinese restaurant around the corner from my place."

"Actually I would love to; let me just call Omar and let him know, hold on."

Using her cell phone she called Omar to let him know she would be hanging with the girls before heading back to his place.

"I'll be there in about twenty minutes" Rachel said to Lorraine as she closed her cell phone to end the call with Omar.

"Okay, I'll see you there bye" replied Lorraine.

Rachel put her things together in her overnight bag, however just as she was about to leave she smelt something but couldn't figure out what it was. She went into to the kitchen and was almost taken aback by the foul odor coming from the garbage. While in the kitchen she decided to wash the dishes considering she wasn't sure when she'd be back. She then grabbed the garbage and headed out the door. When she arrived at the restaurant Lorraine was already there.

"Where's Kim?"

"She just went to the bathroom" Lorraine replied.

"Well I'll be ordering my food to go because Omar will be heading home soon".

Just then the waiter came to take their orders. Lorraine ordered chicken fried rice with chicken balls, while Rachel ordered stirred fried pork with shrimp fried rice, sweet and sour ribs, chicken balls and two egg rolls. Kim came back just in time to order chicken wings with stir fried noodles and an egg roll.

"Can I have my order to go please?" said Rachel.

"Would you ladies like anything to drink while you wait?"

"Yes please can we have a pitcher of Budweiser?" said Kim.

"Will that be all?"

"Yes thank you" said Lorraine.

"So Rachel, why can't you eat with us?" Kim asked.

"I'm going over to Omar's, he's at work right now but I'm meeting him at his place."

"So you and Omar are a couple now?" Kim asked.

"To be honest I'm not sure but it's heading in the right direction and now that I'm no longer married to Roger I can move on with my life."

"Well I like him and you two make a good couple." said Kim.

The waiter came back with their food and told Rachel that she could pick-up her order at the front when she is leaving. They talked until eight-thirty until Rachel said she had to leave.

"Well girl don't be a stranger; give me a call if you're not too busy with your man" said Lorraine.

"Don't worry I won't be too busy besides there is no man that is going to make me forget about my friends. You all where there before he came and you'll be there when he's gone if I need a shoulder to cry on."

"Girl you got nothing to worry about that man isn't going anywhere" said Kim.

"Okay I hope your right bye." Simultaneously Kim and Lorraine said good bye as Rachel made her way to the front desk to pick up her order. Once Rachel left they ordered desert and talked about their upcoming trip to Jamaica for Steveroy's family reunion and made plans to go shopping. They left the restaurant and decided to go to the movies.

CHAPTER EIGHTEEN

VANESSA WAS SO disappointed in herself for not knowing that she was pregnant as Dr. Granger her colleague confirmed what she already knew. Now that it was confirmed she prayed that there was no permanent damage to her unborn child from all the drinking she had done at the party. The doctor took more blood test and handed Vanessa a bottle; once she returned from the bathroom as if she didn't know Dr. Granger told her that it would take three to four days to get the results back to confirm if there was any damage done to the fetus. Vanessa knew that there was no way she could tell Howard that she was pregnant until she was absolutely sure their baby was fine. She left Dr. Grangers office and took the elevator down to the second floor to meet Howard for his appointment with Dr. Patterson.

Howard dread the thought of Vanessa knowing why he had been so tired but the truth had to come to light because his condition was getting worst. It was starting to show that there was something wrong because he was nauseated all the time and had no appetite. Although he had told Vanessa that the appointment was at 11:30 it was actually at 11:15 he wanted to be able to speak with the doctor before she arrived. He wanted to make sure that the doctor didn't tell her how long he knew about his condition. Once in the doctor's office, Dr. Patterson put his mind at ease by letting him know that although he would be in the room he would allow Howard to tell Vanessa but if there were any questions that he wasn't able to answer he would. Vanessa arrived downstairs at 11:25 and called her husband to find out where he was; as she spoke to him on the phone the office door opened and Howard emerged with a smile on his face as he gestured for her to come in. The appointment which was only supposed to last an hour took almost two hour. By the time they left Dr. Patterson's office the waiting room had three patience waiting and the fourth one was expected to arrive any minute. Vanessa was overwhelmed by all the information that she had to take in. She knew that there was no way she would be able to go to work. After telling her receptionist that she had an emergency and had to leave for the day; they both went home. Vanessa was very angry with her husband for keeping such a big secret from her; she couldn't understand why he didn't tell her. After all she was a doctor and she could have helped him understand and deal with his symptoms. The only good thing was that he was taking the erlotinib pills Dr. Patterson prescribe and now she had to convince him how important it was that he try chemotherapy if it wasn't too late.

The results about her pregnancy took longer than it was supposed to but when Vanessa found out that the baby was fine and there was no permanent damage she knew it was time to tell her husband. After finding out that her husband had cancer Vanessa felt like her world was coming to end because there would be no life without him. How was she going to raise three kids by herself, continue to work, pay the bill and manage a mortgage on her own? Keeping that in mind Vanessa went upstairs and told her husband that she was pregnant. With excitement in his eyes Howard hugged his wife and told her how happy he was but she could hear the pain in his voice as he spoke. He was overwhelmed with everything that was going on in his life as tears formed in his eyes. Releasing her he walked over to the closet and started to get dress.

"Where are you going?"

"To Rick's Pub I just need to get out of here."

"Well I thought we could talk about everything Dr. Patterson told me. We can go online and see if there is any alternative medicine that could help you."

"Did you not hear what the doctor said I am going to die, so let's not make this any harder on either one of us? Now if it's okay with you I'm going out".

Vanessa was shocked and hurt by his words as well as his actions. His words were so cold yet she could see the pain in his eyes; so instead of getting on him about it she just let him leave without saying another word. Howard didn't mean to be so cold toward his wife but Tracy was insisting that he meet her at the Pub. She needed to talk to him. In the past three days she had called him fifty-six times, gone by his work and left several threatening messages that she would come to his house if he didn't meet her at the Pub; reluctantly he decided to meet her.

As he drove to the Pub there were a million thoughts going through his mind as to why Tracy wanted to talk to him so badly. He parked close to the front, went inside and walked over to the bar to find Tracy waiting for him. It had been almost four months since the last time he saw Tracy and it was obvious that she was pregnant.

There was no doubt that she was very upset. To keep her calm he brought her over to a booth so that they could talk in private. He tried to calm her down by asking her how she was doing, how far along she was and if she needed anything, but that was the wrong thing to say.

"Do you even know what you're asking me? Of course I need something. I need you to be man enough to face the fact that this is your child."

"How do I know that this is my child; I'm sure I wasn't the only man you were sleeping with?" Shocked by his words Tracy stood up and started yelling at him without a care about anyone else in the pub; Howard gently pulled her back to sit down. After calming her down they were able to continue the conversation and as much as he didn't want to believe it Howard knew in his heart that she wasn't lying to him. He recalled the last time they were together and he remembered that he didn't use a condom.

"I am not trying to ruin your marriage or force you to be a part of my baby's life but I just thought that you would want to know."

"I just want you to know that I'm sorry about everything I said and if you need anything at all, please let me know. Just call me at work. I think you should know that my wife is also pregnant and I really don't need you to cause her any stress."

"What! You're being hard on me because you got both of us pregnant. You have some nerves, you want me to keep my mouth shut so your wife won't be stressed. You act as if I got pregnant by myself. Just so know you were very much involved. So we both need to deal with our situation and if that means your wife knowing I'm pregnant then that's your issue not mine."

"No, that's not it at all. There's just a lot of shit going on in my life right now. It seems that everything is happening all at once. My life is falling apart."

"So, talk to me; you used to tell me your problems before. What's so different now?"

"The only way I'll tell you is if you promise that you won't tell anyone" Howard said.

"I promise."

For the next thirty-five minutes as they talked, he managed to tell her more than he had told his wife. He told her that he had cancer with less than a year to live. With tears in his eyes, he told her that Leroy was dead and he could have saved him. The whole time he was talking, she was looking deep into his eyes to see if he was telling her the truth and he was. She knew him long enough to know when he was lying and this wasn't one of those times. As they continued to talk Howard wanted to tell her about the robbery but he knew that wasn't something he could do. Talking about his problems with Tracy made him feel as if it would make it easier for him to tell his wife now that he got another woman's pregnant. It was going to be hard for him to tell Vanessa but he needed to get it off his chest. Even though it didn't make the situation any better, he felt a great sign of relief afterwards. Tracy was in a state of shock from everything he had just told her. She didn't know what to say or do, so instead, she just held his hand and told him that she would be there for him whenever he needed her.

With that said Howard decided he would call his wife and tell her to come down to the Pub so that they all could talk and he was going to tell her that Tracy was pregnant with his child.

"Do you mean what you just said?" he asked.

"Of course, I do.

"Okay hold on, I'll be right back. Don't move." Howard left the booth and went over to the pay phone. He dialled his home number and told Vanessa to come down to the Pub. When he returned to the booth, he told Tracy what he was about to do and asked her not to let Vanessa know that he already told her he had cancer. Tracy agreed and Howard went to wait for Vanessa by the bar; while waiting for his wife he was a nervous wreck. He knew that telling his wife with Tracy there was not going to be easy but she needed to know the truth. He wasn't doing it to embarrass her in anyway but he felt that the best way to tell her was to show her. When she arrived he told her that there was someone he wanted her to meet. Not knowing what to expect Vanessa wanted to order a double rum and coke with no ice; instead she got a bottle of water. Howard then took her by the hand and led her over to the booth. When she saw Tracy, she pulled her hand away and froze. Howard took hold of her hand again and told her to please have a seat. He introduced them, took a deep breath and told both of them to just listen before they said a word.

"Vanessa the reason I've been so distant is because there is a lot of shit happening right now in my life."

He sat there as if he were in the hot seat and told her everything except about robbing Mr. Edwards because he knew that she would never keep the money if she knew the truth. After telling Vanessa that Tracy was pregnant for him; he then told them he needed to know that they could be friends because he wanted his kids to grow up knowing each other. At this point, he had tears in his eyes and a lump in his throat, leaving him unable to say another word.

CHAPTER NINETEEN

LATER THAT WEEK, Tyrone dropped by to visit Howard, looking like a new man. First of all, he pulled up in a new 98 Jaguar fully loaded, top of the line clothes, as well as a Gucci watch and a diamond ring that almost blinded Howard as Tyrone walked into the house.

"Hey Howard, how are you doing?"

"Oh, I'm alright, I guess but the doctor has me on some strong ass medicine that makes me so sick all the time, but I see you're doing just fine though."

"What's that's supposed to mean!"

"What you can't figure it out because from where I'm standing you are just giving it all away."

"No, but I'm sure you're going to tell me, so spit it out."

"Okay, what the fuck is your problem! Don't you realize how much attention you're drawing to yourself right now? The police already suspect you had something to do with the robbery and shooting, now you're just making it easier for them to put the pieces together!"

"Don't be jealous because you won't be around to enjoy your share and I can."

Tyrone could see the pain and disappointment on Howard's face as he spoke and wished he could take back his words. Howard was his closest friend and he knew within his heart that he was telling him the truth.

"If that's what you want to think, okay but keep in mind that I did warn you and you did promise me that you would keep my name out of it."

"If that's what you're worried about, you don't have to worry, I'll keep my promise to you."

"No that is not all that I'm thinking about do you think I want you to go to jail but if you keep spending money the way you are it's only a matter of time before the police come knocking at your door?"

Although Tyrone knew that Howard was right and he was just looking out for his best interest he didn't want to hear what he had to say; so instead of staying he told Howard he had to go.

Mrs. Anderson was still determined to find out what had happen to her son. All the police could tell her is that it was still under investigation; however after talking to Tyrone she was convinced that he knew more than he was letting on. Without hesitation she picked up the phone and dialed his number and told him she was on her way over. She needed to speak with him face to face so, that she could look him in the eyes and see whether he was lying to her or not. As soon as Tyrone noticed that it was Mrs. Anderson calling his heart started to beat faster, she had been calling him constantly trying to find out more information about Leroy's death. He couldn't deal with her coming over to his place right now because she would definitely want to know where he had gotten the money to buy his new furnisher.

He knew that he shouldn't be spending the money so carelessly but he couldn't help himself. He had grown up with five brothers and three sisters and money was always an issue in his family especially after his father left. His mother struggled to put food on the table, clothes on their back and to keep a roof over their heads, until him and his older brother started selling drugs to help her out. His mother never knew where the money was coming from but she did suspected that her boys where up to no good.

Tyrone nearly jumped out of his seat when he heard the door knock; there was no doubt in his mind that it was Mrs. Anderson. Reluctantly he got up to answer the door.

"Hi Mrs. Anderson, please come in."

Mrs. Anderson had never been to Tyrone's apartment before. However she remembered Leroy saying how old his furnisher was and that he kept his place very messy. As she looked around almost everything she laid her eyes on was new and it was spotless.

"Boy you must have done something wrong, why do look so nervous to see me?"

"Mrs. Anderson you know me better than that I can do no wrong."

"Well then you need to relax I just want to talk to you about Leroy. By the way did you design your place yourself or did you have someone come in and decorate for you?"

"No, I did most of it myself. Do you like what you see because you're the first woman to come here since it's been done?

"Yes it's quite lovely, Leroy used to say that your furnisher needed to be updated when did you have it done?"

"Actually Leroy and I pick out most of the stuff from the Ikea Magazine, the rest I got from Wal-Mart and Pier One. Please have a seat. Would you like something to drink?" She replied no thank you; as she sat on the loveseat.

Lying to Mrs. Anderson about her son was hard but he needed her to believe that he didn't just furnish his apartment.

"How have you been doing?"

"Well if those damn police would get off their asses and find out who killed my son then that would be a great start to my day. You have connections on the streets; haven't you heard anything about what has happened?"

"I want to find out what happened just as badly as you do. As far as I know it was the security guard that shot him."

Just as the words came out of his mouth he knew he shouldn't have said anything.

"So if I hear anything else I will let you know."

"Who said it was the security guard?"

"Well to be honest that's just the word on the street and you know you can't always trust that."

"That's so true but do you think the person that told you would be willing to talk to me or the police about it?"

"Now Mrs. Anderson most of the stuff I hear are from people who don't like the police and will only talk to someone they know but if I hear anything else I will definitely let you know."

"Tyrone darling I've known you almost all your life and I can see that you're hiding something, whatever it is you can tell me."

"Honestly Mrs. Anderson there is nothing else I know, you may think I know something but it's just because I'm still so upset over Leroy's death".

Just then the phone rang and Tyrone was glad as he said "excuse me while I answer this." It was only Howard but Tyrone pretended that it was an important call. He placed the call on hold and Mrs. Anderson he really needed to take this call. She gave him a hug and left.

"What was that all about?"

"Mrs. Anderson was here questioning me about Leroy's death and I just didn't want to continue lying to her so, that's why I pretended you were someone else. I really need to get away from her, she is driving me crazy with all the questions."

"Well just where do you plan on going? Howard said.

"I don't know but really and truly I can't take it anymore. She is calling me at least 3-4 times a day and now today she comes over. What's next?"

"Okay! Then take a vacation but just make sure you don't get on a plane; take a bus or train."

Twenty minutes later Tyrone hung up the phone with Howard. Then called his cousin Rocco to asked him if he could come stay with him. While packing his bag he called Howard; told him he was going to stay with his cousin and then headed for the bus station.

Howard was glad Tyrone was leaving town, he had been very careless with his spending and who knows what else. Mrs. Anderson had called him a few times as well but he had obviously made her believe that he knew nothing about Leroy's death. she had stopped calling after two weeks. Vanessa on the other hand was harder to convince because she still questioned him about that night. She just didn't believe that he knew nothing, considering he never really gave her a proper answer about where he and Tyrone were that night and why Leroy wasn't with them.

CHAPTER TWENTY

THE NEXT MORNING just as Kim was about to leave for work the phone rang.

"Hello" Although she knew it was her mother Kim couldn't make out a word she was saying, this caused her to panic because her mother was crying hysterically.

"Mom what's wrong?"

"It's your uncle Ronny, he's been in an accident, and we need to get to the hospital because they don't know if he's going to make it, can you come get me I can't do this alone."

Just hearing her uncle's name made her skin crawl. He had sexually abused her when she was twelve, made her believe that no man would want her unless she slept with them. He then threatened her so, she would keep her mouth shut. Throughout the years she had avoid all contact with him and never told anyone what he had done or how much she hated him. His words had rang load in her head with every man she met, and she always hoped that once she slept with them they would actually want to be with her. However, it never worked out that way because no man wants a woman that sleeps with them too soon.

"Honey, are you still there?" her mother asked.

"Yes mom I'm still here but I was just on my way to work, can't someone else bring you to the hospital?"

Kim knew as soon as the words came out it was the wrong thing to say. However her feelings for her uncle ran deep.

"Kimberly James! Your uncle is dying and all you can think about is going to work. I know that you haven't been very close with your uncle but I would sure hope that you would at least want to say bye to him."

As her mother spoke she could hear the pain in her voice so, she told her that she would be there as soon as possible. Once she hung up Kim dialed her office and inform her secretary that she may not be coming in but if she needed her she could be reached on her cell phone. Although she didn't want her mother to arrive late to say good bye to her twin brother, Kim was in no rush to get to her mother's place. Half an hour later she stood outside her uncle's hospital room and refused to go in.

After what he had put her through, the thought that she could over power him while he laid on his death bed made her realize that there was no way she could go in there. She wanted to beat the shit out of him; over power him like he had done to her and as much as her mother begged her to go into the room with her; she just couldn't. She was glad when her aunt Josephine arrived and went into the room with her mother. By noon the whole James clan had arrive and precisely at three fifteen Ronny Clifton James was pronounced dead. There was a huge outburst of crying and screaming as the doctor informed everyone, even Kim was crying but unlike everyone else she cried for other reason. She had to force herself from not smiling or laughing out loud.

One week later he was buried beside his mother, with his father on the opposite side. With her uncle gone Kim felt that she could finally tell her mother but she knew she would have to wait awhile, so instead she to tell her cousin Brenda, uncle Ronny's eldest daughter because she had always been someone she could talk to.

A week after the funeral Kim invited her cousin over and with a bottle of Bacardi and several cans of coke she managed to let it all out. However, she was shocked when Brenda confessed that he had been doing the same thing to her too and that if she had known he was also doing it to Kim she would have had the strength to tell her mother. They both decided that it would only cause both their mothers pain to know the truth so; they came to the conclusion to keep it between themselves. It was their dirty little secret but Kim couldn't help but thinking if there was anyone else he had done it to.

CHAPTER TWENTY-ONE

IT HAD BEEN a month since Howard told Vanessa about Tracy and still she wasn't able to find the right words to say to her husband, even though they had gone to see his doctor twice. She didn't know whether to be mad because he got another woman pregnant, or should she be mad because he was dying. For weeks, he had been sleeping on the couch but she needed him back in their bed. She hated the distance between them, the baby was moving so much and she wanted to share that with him. Whenever the kids asked him why he was on the couch, he told them he was catching a cold and didn't want to give it to mommy. Which was the truth, the cancer was taking a toll on his body. It's true what they say when it rains it pours. Three days later, on the answering machine, Tyrone left a message.

"Howard, I'm at the police station. I need you to bail me out. Where the fuck are you! They want ten thousand dollars for bail. Come quick."

Tyrone didn't get very far before he was picked up at the bus station by the police. Being placed in handcuffs for the first time was very uncomfortable considering the officer had no sympathy when putting them on. By the time Howard received the message it was too late to call the police station to make bail. However he was shocked the next morning when Tianna brought him the morning paper. On the front page was a picture of Tyrone and the headline read. 'Suspect found in the senseless murder of three men also known to be a friend of the employee of Mr. Edwards. Howard hoped Vanessa didn't see the paper, but that was just wishful thinking. She asked him if he had anything to do with it since they were together that night but he lied and it sounded better than he thought it would because she believed his story. He then told her that he was going to the police station and she insisted that she come because of his condition.

When they arrived at the station it was packed. There were five to six guys in handcuffs and shackles. There were two lines of people waiting to be served and others were sitting down. He didn't know whether to sit or wait in one of the lines, so he asked one of the ladies sitting down. She told him to wait in the line on the left and then he would be sent to the line on the right, after that he would be able to sit down. She then told him that if he was here to bail someone he would be here for awhile. She was right because four hours later Howard's name was finally called. He filled out the paper work which took another fifteen minutes and on top of that a police officer came over and asked him more questions, took the papers from him and then asked him his name. Howard's first thought was to tell him to look on the damn paper, but of course he didn't say that.

"Howard Terrence Blackwood."

"And how were you able to come up with this amount of money?" the officer asked.

"As I wrote on the paper, I do have a job. As well my wife is a doctor. Half of the money came from my account and the other half from hers and feel free to check it out, we'll wait."

"That won't be necessary." The officer then led Howard into the waiting room, told him to take a seat because it would be at least an half an hour before Mr. Davis would be release.

Forty-five minutes later Tyrone walked out accompanied by another police officer, with more papers for Howard to sign so Tyrone could be released. As Howard read over the papers it stated that Tyrone was being released into his custody and if he didn't appear in court on May 27, which was just four weeks away, he would be held liable. Not only that, the money he posted for bail would be taken and he would be fined. As well there would be a warrant out for Tyrone's arrest. Howard signed the papers and they walked out of the police station with Tyrone trailing behind. Once home, they allowed Vanessa to go inside so, that they could talk. Howard didn't want to say a word even though he was boiling inside with anger. He was pissed at how stupid Tyrone was and still hurting inside at the loss of his best friend. Tyrone on the other hand, just kept bragging.

"The police have nothing on me. Just because I'm spending money, that doesn't mean that I had anything to do with the robbery. I do have a job." To top it off he wanted Howard to tell the police that he had given him some money as a loan, and for that split second, Howard could see the fear in Tyrone's eyes, it was fear of going to jail. Of course, he felt sorry for him, but he was more worried about him keeping his mouth shut rather than his fear of going to jail. Before he got a chance to answer, Vanessa came outside to let Howard know she was going to bed. Howard already knew what his answer would be but instead, he told Tyrone he'd think about it and let him know in the morning.

CHAPTER TWENTY-TWO

WHEN RACEL WALKED into her office ten minutes late she was surprised to see everyone standing around like they had nothing better to do. They all said good morning as if they were waiting all morning for her to arrive. So, instead of inquiring why, she said good morning, walked into her office and closed the door. When she turned around, there were twelve dozen roses on her desk and a card. Knowing it must be from Omar; she rushed over to her desk, smelt the roses and picked up the card.

"This is to inform you that as of three o'clock today, you are on a four day vacation with someone who loves you very much. Don't ask where we're going. I'll pick you up at two-thirty in front of the building so we can go shopping and don't worry about your office they will manage without you. I've already told everyone, love always Omar".

Rachel found it hard to concentrate on her work. She kept looking at the roses and wondering where he was taking her so she called him. However, the only information he would give her was that they were going on an island and then he hung up the phone. When she called him back, he just said, "Love you bye." At two twenty she was so excited she packed up her things and got ready to leave. She then printed her report, made a copy for her file and another one for her receptionist to mail out to the client before she left.

At exactly three, Omar arrived with a big smile on his face as he got out of the car to open the door for her. He bent over and gave her a long, meaningful kiss, leaving her weak in the knees and her body waiting more. He opened the door and helped her inside the car.

"So, what do you have up your sleeves?"

"You're just going have to wait and find out babes."

"Why won't you tell me where we're going?"

"It's a surprise. That's why."

"Then, can you at least tell me what the occasion is?"

"It's to celebrate our six months back together anniversary, starting from the first time we had sex again."

"You actually remembered that day?"

"Of course, how could I forget? That's the day I told you I loved you again."

Rachel was shocked that he would remember something like that especially because she didn't. She leaned over, gave him a kiss and then told him how much she loved him before they drove off. Packing for their long weekend was more work than they both thought it would be. Everything they saw was something they needed for their trip. After their shopping spree, he took her out for an early dinner.

Before heading to Omar's place they stopped by Rachel's to pick up some personal items and the rest of her clothes. When they got to his place he set the bath for her, undressed her and allowed her to relax while he sent an email to his assistant Anthony. Omar was glad to be going away with Rachel but very nervous because he would be making his decision whether he wanted to ask her to marry him or not. He was ready to make a commitment and settle down after all he wasn't getting any younger. Once that was done he took a quick shower in the other bathroom and fell asleep naked on his bed.

Thirty minutes later Rachel emerged from the bathtub, wrapped a towel around herself and went into the room to find Omar sleeping naked on top of the sheets. Looking down at his naked body as he laid on his back aroused her; she then walked around to his side of the bed and took hold of his manhood. She held his limp pleasure stick in her hand and ran her tongue up and down the length of it; within seconds Omar was rock hard. She then wrapped his swollen manhood in a warmth of pleasure as she took him in her mouth.

"Oh baby that feels so good".

"Yeah you like that?"

"Yes I do. Please don't stop baby."

"Mmm you taste so good and if you don't want me to stop then taste me?"

She didn't have to say another word to convince him as he allowed her to position herself on top of him so that her sweetness was in his face. Tasting her honey on his tongue almost drove him mad; he had no problem eating with his fingers as he slid one then two finger inside of her. Her orgasm was at its peak when Omar sat up; put her in the doggie style position and entered her with a forceful hunger. He grabbed onto her hair as she begged for him to fuck her harder; with every stroke her moans enticed him to go deeper. Several positions later Rachel's hair was a hot mess and Omar was exhausted in a pool of sweat.

By the time they were done it made no sense to go to sleep because it was almost time to get ready to go to the airport. Their flight was leaving at two o'clock in the morning. It was the best flight he could get on such short notice but the good thing was that they would be there by eight o'clock the next morning; so instead of going to sleep they took a shower together and got dressed.

CHAPTER TWENTY-THREE

THE NEXT MORNING Vanessa and Kim met at Starbucks for coffee. Leaving Howard alone with Tyrone worried her but she needed to get out of the house. Vanessa knew that her husband and Tyrone were hiding something but since neither one wanted to tell her what was going on she decided she didn't want to be around them. Ever since the night of their house warming party, so many things had changed: Leroy was dead, she found out that Howard had cancer, another woman was pregnant for her husband and now Tyrone was being accused of being in involved with the death of his friend. To make matters worse she couldn't help feeling that Howard knew more about Leroy's death than he was telling her.

When Vanessa arrived at Starbucks, she was not in the best of moods but it was nice to have someone to talk to. She told Kim everything that had happened the night before and then she allowed Kim to do what she did best; which was talk about herself. As much as Vanessa wanted to block her out, she couldn't because she couldn't believe half the stuff that was coming out of her mouth.

"What do you mean you think you love Richard? Didn't you just say that about the last guy that you were sleeping with?"

"I know; but he always wants to spend time with me, and he is so sensitive and caring towards me." Vanessa continued to listen to her in shock until she couldn't take it anymore.

"Are you hearing what you're saying? First of all, you said he mostly comes over at night, not in the day. He never calls unless he wants to come over which is always late at night and he hardly takes you out. You have never met any of his family and to top it off you only have his work number, when everyone and their grandmother has a cell phone nowadays. Can you not see that there is something very wrong with this picture?"

"I know and we have talked about all of that and he explained everything plus the only reason we only see each at night is because we are both so busy during the days. He has taken me away for long weekends and honestly we don't even have sex every time we are together so don't make it seem like it's only about the sex."

"Don't get me wrong Kim; I'm not trying to cut him down but he is a married man. If you're not willing to stop sleeping him enjoy it for what it is and see other guys. Only time can tell if he feels the same way as you do. It seems to me that you're rushing to find love, but true love comes to you and you'll know when you've found it."

"So, why is it so easy for you, your sister, Lorraine and everyone else around me to find love, but not me?"

"We didn't go looking for it; it came to us. Plus, when we did find love, we made sure it was a two way street, not one way. You make it too obvious, that's what you're looking for whenever you meet someone. Guys take that as a weakness and also take advantage of the situation."

"How do I make it look too obvious?"

"First of all you give it up too soon and then you expect the guy to stick around. You believe everything they tell you, while giving them your all and getting nothing in return. I'm not saying you shouldn't work hard at a relationship, but keep in mind it should be fifty-fifty, not you giving one hundred percent."

"You just don't seem to understand I really believe that Richard is the one. Haven't you seen the way he is when we're together?"

"Well like I said don't get me wrong Kim, I'm not saying that there may or may not be something there but just don't rush into it because I don't want you to get hurt."

"I understand what you're saying and I'm going to ask him to come to Jamaica with me and see what his answer will be."

"Kim how do you expect a married man to get away for a week?"

"I don't know but hopefully if he cares he will find a way to come with me."

"Well I hope it all works out for you because you deserve it girl."

They sat talking for an hour until Kim thought it was time she went home considering she had to take the bus because her car was in the shop again. On her way home she called Richard and asked him if he could come over because she wanted to talk to him; reluctantly he agreed and told her he would be there in 45mins. When Kim arrived home she made sure that her apartment was spotless, as nice as Richard was he could be very anal at times. She often wondered how his wife put up with him and was glad that she was only with him temporary. One hour later Richard let himself into her apartment with his keys. As he walked in he yelled out.

"Hi babes."

Startled by his voice Kim told him she would be right out. While she was off in her bedroom he rolled up a joint; he loved the effect it had on her because she was always willing to do, so much more when she was high. When Kim walked into the living room the sweet smell of marijuana filled the air. She was wearing nothing but heels and holding her treasure box where she kept all of her sex toys. Richard face lit up when he seen the box because he knew without a doubt that they were going to have a great time. Although, Richard loved his wife, there was nothing like an affair with a very sexual woman like Kim. She did things his wife won't even consider doing. So many times he tried to convince his wife to try new things but she always refused. She had complained that he wanted her to do things she wasn't comfortable doing. Even after he told her he wanted a freak in the bedroom and a lady on the streets she still wouldn't do the things he liked.

Kim walked over to him and put the box on the table; she then turned around and jiggled her ass in his face while bending over so he could get a full view of her sweetness. Richard then grabbed her by the hips, pulled her closer and nestled his face between her legs. As she squirmed to get away he held on tight to her hips while tickling her with his tongue. Her moans and giggles could be heard throughout the apartment as he continued to enjoy her sweet nectar. Kim's pleasure was at its peak as her body erupted in his face; her legs gave way and she fell to the floor. Richard put out his hand for her and she took it as he pulled her to sit beside him on the couch; he then passed her the joint and the lighter. After lighting the joint, Kim asked Richard if he would come with her to Jamaica. To her surprise he didn't say no, he agreed to come but he would only be able to stay from Friday to Monday instead of the whole week. For the next couple of days Lorraine and Kim went shopping to get everything they needed for their trip on Monday. Even though, she would only be staying for a week, Kim was extremely thrilled Richard agreed to come to Jamaica with her. He was catching an early flight on Friday morning and they would be leaving together Monday night. He gave her two thousand dollars to buy whatever she needed and to pick up a few things for him. Kim didn't waste any time spending his money to get everything she needed for their trip. Everything she bought was expensive: from the matching suitcases, new bathing suits, sandals, shorts, summer dresses; right down to the four matching bras and panties. By Sunday afternoon she had packed both their suitcase and was waiting for Richard to come over for dinner.

Kim was overwhelmed with excitement when Richard dropped her off at the airport; knowing that he would be meeting her in Jamaica. She met up with Lorraine and Steveroy, checked in and waited to board the plane. Throughout the entire flight they talked about all the different places Steveroy would be taking them. The flight attendant announced that they were about to descend; so everyone needed to fasten their seatbelts and put their seats in an upright position. Lorraine alone with many other passengers began to scream and clap as the plane was about to land.

Once they landed, they went to locate their luggage. When they left the airport Steveroy's cousin Tommy was waiting outside for them in a blue 350 Lexus SUV.

From the moment Tommy laid eyes on Kim he wanted her and it was obvious by the way his manhood made a tent inside his track pants. He was glad that she came alone until his cousin told him her man was coming too in a couple of days. When they arrived at his house which looked more like a mansion Tommy showed them to their rooms and told them dinner would be ready in three hours. He helped Kim with her luggage and convinced her to put on her bathing suit and come to the pool with him. After getting him to leave her room. She plow through her suitcase for her one piece bathing suit and went into the bathroom to change.

For the next two hours they sat talking and he realized that they had a lot in common which turned him on even more. Kim was glad that she didn't go into the pool when the cook announced that dinner was ready. Dinner was very exquisite with: fish, lobster, shrimps, roast chicken, plain rice, rice peas, sweet potatoes, macaroni pie, mix vegetable, both garden and Caesars salad. After dinner the four of them went down to the beach with blankets, weed and a bottle of Jamaicans well known Wray & Nephew Rum. As interested in Kim as Tommy was he wanted to know more about the older women his cousin had falling in love with and had brought to their family reunion. Lorraine was surprised that Tommy was talking more to her than Kim but it became obvious that he was fishing for information about her either for himself or his cousins.

Tommy took them on many tours of the island and they partied every night. On Thursday they went to Rick's Café in Ocho Rios and then to Amnesia night club. They partied until early in the morning and decided that it would be best to leave from the club and pick Richard up from the airport. Kim was so excited that Richard was finally coming because she felt that their relationship was moving in the right direction now that he was filing for a divorce.

The reunion wasn't until Sunday. So, Tommy decided to invite his girlfriend to come with them to the Bob Marley Museum because he didn't want feel like a fifth wheel. Throughout the day the couples separated and Lorraine, Kim and Tommy's girlfriend Michelle was able to have some alone time while the guys were off doing manly stuff. The next day Lorraine was shocked to see how big Steveroy's family was, never mind everyone wasn't even able to come. They had a great time at the reunion; there was almost five hundred family and friends. Lorraine got to meet Steveroy's twin sister, two brothers along with his father and grandparents.

After Kim and Richard left Lorraine spent the next few days getting to know Steveroy's parents, sibling and rest of his family. She felt as if she had known them most of her life because they all made her feel so comfortable. They toured Jamaica and the night before Lorraine and Steveroy was leaving Tommy took them to Pier One the hottest night club in Montego Bay and eight hours later they were on a plane heading home.

CHAPTER TWENTY-FOUR

RACHEL AND OMAR arrived at the Cayman International Airport and grabbed a cab to The Ritz Carlton hotel. It was a twenty minute trip but for Omar it seemed to take forever because he was dead tired. Rachel, on the other hand, was glad she slept on the plane because she wanted to enjoy every moment as she snapped picture all the way to the hotel. After checking in, they both decided that Omar would take a nap while Rachel took care of the agenda for the rest of their Vacation.

After unpacking their luggage, she checked out their hotel room which was very beautiful. It was the biggest hotel room she had ever seen. It even had a kitchen with a fully stocked refrigerator. She then brought their things into the bedroom, which took her aback. It had wall to wall mirrors, a king size bed, TV, fireplace and then there was the bathroom which had the biggest Jacuzzi she ever saw. There was also a stand up shower and his and hers sinks; it was bigger than her whole bedroom. When she was finished, she went down to the lobby to check out the place. She picked up many brochures so she would be able to find the best sights to see while in the Cayman Island and went back upstairs. Omar was still asleep, so she lay beside him and rested.

Two hours later, Omar was awakened by the phone. It was room service asking if they wanted anything for dinner. Omar was shocked that he had slept so long. Instead he asked the man if she could arrange for a cab to bring them to the best restaurant in town in an hour. He thanked the man, and woke Rachel up to get ready. They took a nice long hot shower together, got dressed, grabbed the camera and left after the front desk called up to let them know the cab was waiting. The cab driver pulled up in front of the Agua Restaurant and Lounge, once seated they ordered crab portobello and lobster rolls appetizers. For dinner they ordered herb crusted rack of lamb and stuff chicken breast, as they shared each other's food with a bottle of chardonnay.

After dinner they decided to go back to the hotel and check out what kind of entertainment was available; they ended up at the hotel night club and danced provocatively on the dance floor as all eyes were on them. As they held hands and strolled back to their room every nerve end in Rachel's body was tingling; her feeling for Omar was overwhelming. To exhausted from the dancing and drinking they both fell asleep without even taken a shower.

The next morning after breakfast they swam with the dolphins and went to the Casanova Restaurant for Italian cuisine. Although Rachel felt the need to check in with work and her family being with Omar made her overlook the need to do that. She was the happiest she had ever been, glad that her divorce was final and she could move on with her life. Even though Roger had sent her several letters from jail, each time she just threw them out not even reading one of them. Omar on the other hand had purchased an engagement ring and was just waiting for the right moment to ask her to be his wife.

On the third day they went on a tour to see the Cayman Motor Museum which was a unique attraction that featured an 1886 Benz that was the very first automobile ever produced. Rachel was surprised and impressed that she had such a good time at the museum.

Once back in their hotel room they went into the shower together and Omar washed every inch of Rachel's body. The sweet sensation of his hands on her body was torture because every time she tried to touch him he slapped her hand away. He then stepped out of the shower and told her that he would be waiting for her on the bed. When she came out of the bathroom with the towel wrapped around her he told her to drop the towel. He then instructed her to put on the blindfold that was on the edge of the bed. She did as she was told and once it was on he pulled her onto the bed; and laid her on her stomach. Omar poured Making Love massage oil vanilla flavor into his hands, rub his hands together and worked it into her body. He worked the muscles in her neck, shoulders, back and then gently massaged her ass; then turned her over and starting with her feet he worked his way up. When he reached her inner thighs, with both hands he worked the muscles and as he tasted her she moaned for more. As soon as his lips touched her again Rachel's hands reached out but he grabbed both of them and told her not to touch him or he would stop. Not wanting him to stop she placed her hands behind her head and fought the urge to touch him. Making his way to her arms, then her breast he massaged and knead her body into submission. Her breathing was untamed, her moans ear piercing and her body squirmed under his touch. His dick was rock hard as he opened her legs as wide as they would go and she felt the sweet sensation of his full lips assaulting her pussy. While her pussy was being devoured, she then felt his big hands cupping her breast and the beast was unleash.

Rachel's body exploded out of control and for the first time she squirted, it was an unbelievable experience that left her pussy lips swollen. After getting her something to drink and allowing her to recover Omar positioned her in the back shot position and started to smack and squeeze her ass. She then felt him enter her pussy and she moaned from the pleasure his dick was about to give her. With his hands he held onto her hips and started to bang his dick deeper and deeper inside her pussy. Not being able to see his face turned her on even more, Rachel then told him to stop and she got on top of him. She wanted to take control and enjoy every inch of him inside of her as she rode him. Their sexually noise messed into one as they moaned, grunted and screamed obscene words at each other. Rachel felt like she was about to lose her mind, her body squirmed, vibrated and was just out of control as she completely lost count of how many times she come. As Omar released his load inside her he remembered that he didn't put a condom on as they both clasped onto the bed. Not knowing if Rachel would be happy to be pregnant; he knew that he would love for her to have his baby as he drifted off the sleep. Three hours later they were fully energized and ready for dinner; so they took a shower separately this time, got dressed and went for dinner at a nearby restaurant.

After having a lovely dinner, Rachel just couldn't figure out what was up with Omar. He kept getting up to talk to the waiter, and then he would be on the hotel phone. When she asked him who he was talking to, he said.

"You'll see. Just wait."

Instead of going straight to the hotel, they went for a walk along the beach. Omar pulled up his pants, they both took off their shoes and Rachel lifted her dress as they walked in the water. It was a lovely night and the moon was shining bright with a warm breeze. With a plan in mind, Rachel asked him one more time what he was up to, but she got the same reply.

"Oh so you won't tell me?"

"That's right my love."

"Okay"

With one swift movement, she pushed him into the water and ran. Before she could get very far, he was up and after her. He caught her and tackled her to the ground. They played in the water for awhile before going back to the docks to call a cab to the hotel. Once in the hotel lobby Omar used the phone again. Before going back to their room Omar told Rachel to wait down in the lobby and he would be right back. So she did, but not without wondering what the hell he was up to. Ten minutes later, one of the hotel attendants walked over to her and told her it was okay for her to go upstairs now. She took the elevator and was almost scared to open the door, when she finally did she was taken aback.

As she walked into the room, it was filled with candles, rose pedals on the floor and Omar was nowhere in sight. She followed the pedals to the bedroom and he was on the bed in silk pajamas. Directly in front of the bed was a video camera, then on the night stand was a bowl of melted chocolate and another bowl with strawberries. She continued to walk towards him, but he told her to stop. So, that she could turn on the camera, the music and then slowly remove her clothes. While she did as she was told, he rolled up a joint and made drinks for them as he watched her through the corner of his eyes. Slowly removing her clothes, Rachel moved her hips in a very seductive way. By the time she was naked; Omar was smoking and watching her with a big grin on his face. Rachel continued dancing and every so often she would bend over and show him all of her glory.

"Come her babes and stop teasing me with that sweet pussy." he said.

Rachel needed no convincing as she made her way over to him and took the joint from his hand. He watched as she inhaled the smoke through her mouth and let it out through her nose. She then took one last pull, passed it to him and then she started to pleasure him with her mouth. From the noises he was making there was no doubt that Omar was enjoying every minute of her performance. He then told her that he wanted to taste her sweetness. She positioned herself on her back and the moment his lips touched her, she allowed herself to completely give in to him. They then got into the sixty-nine position until neither one of them could take it anymore.

She then grabbed the bowl of strawberries and stated to eat them one by one from off of his body teasing him with her tongue. Putting a strawberry into her mouth along with his manhood and very skillfully she rolled the strawberry around in her mouth as she gently squeezed. She could feel his body tighten ever time she put pressure on the strawberry, but she continued to do this until he couldn't take it any longer. Omar was so, excited that it scared him. As much as he wanted her to continue, he just couldn't take it. Not knowing if or when she might slip and bite into him instead of the strawberry. He got up and put her into the doggie style position. He then kept smacked her on the ass while talking dirty to her. Her screams could be heard outside of their room but it only motivated him to give it to her even harder. Rachel watched herself on the TV as their every move was being recorded. Seeing herself in action made her feel like she was making a porno movie which was a big turn on.

CHAPTER TWENTY-FIVE

IT WAS AFTER twelve and Vanessa laid waiting on the couch for her husband who was watching Face Off on pay TV at Rick's Pub. Tyrone refused Howard offer to watch the game and was working on a cross word puzzle. Finding it hard to keep her eyes open, Vanessa decided it was time to go to bed. She turned off the TV and went upstairs. Within ten minutes, she was fast asleep.

Half an hour later, Howard pulled into his driveway. Just as he took his seatbelt off he felt a sharp pain in his chest, he felt light headed and was unable to move. In a state of panic, he tried to get out of the car, but instead, he blacked out, hitting the steering wheel and sounding off the horn. Howard lay unconscious with foam coming out of his mouth for three minutes before Bill, his next door neighbor, heard the horn. Thank God for the noisy neighbor because he came out to see what was going on. His first thought when he saw Howard was that he was dead, he then tried to open the car door, but it was locked, so he tried the other doors and they were also locked. He then ran into his house and called 911. Afterwards, he went over to get Vanessa. He rang the doorbell several times and waited but no one answered. So he continued ringing the bell and then he started to bang on the door. Just then the door swung opened and Tyrone was standing their but because Bill didn't know who he was; he was taken aback.

Vanessa thought she heard the doorbell, but figured if it was Howard, he must have his keys since he did drive, so she went back to sleep. Bill informed Tyrone of what was going on and they both rushed over to the car. Before Tyrone was able to find something to break the glass the ambulance arrived and one of the attendant told him that they would handle it.

"The doors are locked" Bill yelled out.

They then broke the back window on the passenger side and opened the door. While they were doing that Tyrone ran back into the house to wake Vanessa. Not wanting to just open the door Tyrone banged on the bedroom door. Vanessa was startled still half asleep, she sat up in her bed and she could see the flashing lights through the window.

"What!"

"Vanessa you need to come now something is wrong with Howard." Before he could finish, she was at the door with her rub half on half off. By this time, they had Howard inside the ambulance. When she ran downstairs and opened the door; the lights nearly blinded her as she ran towards the ambulance.

"What's wrong with him?"

"We don't know yet. We need to get him to the hospital as soon as possible. Are you his wife?"

"Yes, I'm also a doctor at Toronto General and I would like you to bring him there, I just need to grab my purse."

By the time they drove off Vanessa had completely taken over and was telling them what to do. When they arrived at the hospital, Howard was still unconscious, so they gave him a full examination. Several hours later, the doctors couldn't figure out why he wouldn't wake up. Vanessa was so hysterical that the doctor suggested that she go lie down because she was pregnant. She took his advice and one of the nurses took her to an empty room to rest. Before lying down, she called home to check on the kids. She was grateful that Tyrone was there to watch the girls. She then tried calling her sister, but there was no answer so, she left a message for her to call her as soon as she got the message. After three days of shock, Vanessa's mind was at ease. Howard had woken the day before and was able to go home later that day only because Vanessa was a doctor. The doctors knew she would be able to take good care of him at home along with the medication they gave her. Since she was in her last month and she was only working part-time. They also assigned a day nurse to help her because she needed to rest as well. Vanessa thought it would be best if the kids didn't see their father like this, so she had Tyrone take them to Ms. Bedford's for a couple of days.

The whole time she was at the hospital, she tried to get a hold of her sister. It wasn't until Monday that she finally called her office, only to find out that she was taking a few days off, and they didn't know where she could be reached. Rachel didn't even let her know that she was leaving but at the same time she wasn't obligated to tell her everything that was going on in her life.

By noon, Howard was ready to be released, so the ambulance took Vanessa and him home. They set up everything in the living room, so that he wouldn't have to go up and down the stairs. Once Howard was settled in Vanessa walked the ambulance attendants to the door. Just as she close the door the phone rang, she wasn't going to answer it but she thought it might be her sister.

"Hello."

"Hi, is this Mrs. Blackwood?"

Vanessa couldn't place the voice.

"Yes, may I ask who this is?"

With hesitation in her voice, she said,

"Its Tracy, Howard introduced us at Rick's Pub. I'm sorry to bother you, but I heard about what happened, and I just wanted to know if he is okay?"

Vanessa was outraged that her husband's mistress had the nerve to call the house, but it wasn't completely her fault. Howard was more to blame than she was. Instead of being rude to Tracy, she told her that he was doing much better. She also invited her over for dinner tomorrow night so, that they would be able to talk.

"Did you need me to bring anything?" Tracy asked.

"No, that won't be necessary. I'll take care of everything." replied Vanessa.

"How about I bring something for dessert, it's the least I can do?"

"Okay, that would be fine. Can you come around eight?"

Tracy agreed, they said good-bye and Vanessa hung up. She then went into the living room to check on Howard, he was still fast asleep. While she looked at her husband sleeping she wished that she had not invited Tracy over for dinner. Her heart was filled with anger as Howard's words replayed in her head. He had a lot of nerves asking her to be friends with his mistress. However, if this was what he wanted she would find the strength within herself to look beyond her pain. After straightened up the living room, Vanessa grabbed the baby monitor and went upstairs to take a bath before heading to bed. Tracy on the other hand was shocked when Vanessa asked her to come over for dinner. There was no way she could turn down the offer considering she really wanted to see how Howard was doing. She also felt that if she did say no, Vanessa might take it as an insult. She decided to make one of her famous cheese cake but didn't have everything she needed so Tracy went to the grocery store before going to bed.

The next day while the nurse was with Howard; Vanessa went to Mrs. Bedford's to visit the girls and bring them some more clothes. By the time she got home she decided that there was no way she was going to cook for Tracy; so she ordered Chinese food.

CHAPTER TWENTY-SIX

ALHOUGH, IT WAS nice that the kids were staying at the baby-sitter's until Howard felt better. Tyrone felt like he was already in prison, the house was too quite. He couldn't even go outside since Howard was too sick to leave and he was the only person he was allowed to leave the house with. So, he invited his ex-girlfriend Michelle over all the time. Vanessa wasn't too happy about it but she put up with it only because she felt sorry for him. Tyrone prayed that the police wasn't still watching him now that he was only spending the money on drugs. His drug habit had gotten pretty bad; at first he was only drinking; then came the sleeping pills and now he was using cocaine. Tyrone paid Michelle for sex and to bring him the drugs. It worked out just fine for her because she was also using and she did enjoyed having sex when she was high. Every since the robbery, Tyrone was having difficulty sleeping. He kept seeing Leroy in his dreams. He blamed himself for everything that had happened because it was his idea and his fault Leroy died. He remembered how persistent he was that they carried a gun, so that they could have each other's back. However when it came down to it, he was the one that didn't have Leroy's back. He kept having the same dream over and over again. Every time he closed his eyes, Leroy would be standing at the foot of his bed, saying,

"Why didn't you cover me? You were supposed to cover me?" Tyrone would wake up in a pool of sweat, screaming,

"I'm so sorry! Oh, God! I'm so sorry. I know it was my fault."

Since he was staying at Howard's he was afraid of falling asleep because he didn't want to have to explain his dreams to Vanessa. The cocaine allowed him to stay up during the nights, so that he could sleep during the day, while she was at work. Whenever he wasn't sleeping, he drank and took the pills, so that he wouldn't be reminded about the dreams. It was hard for him to sleep during the day. With the amount of drug, alcohol and other things that he had bought; his half of the money was diminishing quickly. He had even gotten his ex-girlfriend Michelle to sell the jewelry on the street but it was hard to get a good price because the word was out about the robbery. No one wanted to touch any of it. Within a short period of time Tyrone's habit was out of control, he feared leaving the room because Vanessa might question him.

CHAPTER TWENTY-SEVEN

RACHEL AND OMAR'S trip was coming to an end, so she thought it was time she did something special for him. She went down to the front desk to talk to Shane, the desk clerk to ask for his help.

"Hi Shane, how are you doing?"

"I'm fine and you?"

"I'm great, but I need to ask you a favor. Would you be able to help me surprise my boyfriend tonight for dinner? Rachel said."

"What do you need me to do?"

"I need you to arrange a candlelight dinner for two on the beach, with a tent, music and a waiter. Would that be a problem?"

"When do you want it to be ready for?"

"Around seven-thirty, we're going to the theater, so can it be ready when we get back?"

"Yes that will not be a problem?" She went back up to the room to find Omar sitting on the couch, watching TV.

"Why aren't you dressed? Did you forget we're going out tonight?" said Rachel.

"So where have you been?"

"It's a surprise and if you want to know you first have to get dressed." He got up and slowly moved towards her with a smile on his face; she knew he was up to something so she headed for the room. He ran behind her and just as she was about to close the door it was too late. He tackled her onto the bed and started to tickle her.

"Tell me what the surprise is?"

"No! You have to wait."

He continued to tickle her, hoping that she would give in, but she didn't, so he decided to do as he was told and get dress.

They spent a wonderful evening at the theater and the whole night Omar was so anxious to find out what the big secret was instead of asking her he kept hinting to her.

"That was a great play. Now what are we going to do?"

"I'll find something. Don't you worry? Let's just walk along the beach for now."

"Then what are we going to do?"

"You'll see."

They both took their shoes off as they walked along the shore, hand in hand; talking about how much fun they'd been having on their trip. It was late and the only light was coming from the moon and the hotel. However, Omar could see some kind of light up ahead but he couldn't figure out exactly what it was. As they continued to walk, the vision became clear. It was a tent set on the beach with lights inside. It was beautiful.

"I wonder what they're doing in there. We should go and take a look." Rachel said.

Omar had no idea that it was part of his surprise but he fell right into the trap.

"Maybe it's a private party. You're not just going to walk in there are you?" asked Omar.

"I would knock, but there's no door. Anyways, we're only going to take a peak. They won't even see us." As they walked closer Omar's heart raced with the excitement of seeing inside the tent. Rachel told him to slowly open the curtain to the tent. As he did, she pushed herself up against him, causing him to go further inside. Just then Shane came up from behind them.

"Can I help you, or did you want to go in?" Omar turned around to see Shane smiling as if it was nothing.

"Go in." Rachel said. They both walked in with Shane right behind them. Just then, Rachel turned to him and said,

"Surprise honey this it all for you to show you how much I love you." The inside was even more beautiful than the outside. There was a blow up bed, a little table and lights all around.

"You did all this for me" he said.

"Yes, you are worth it, aren't you?"

"Of course I am. I'm glad you noticed."

Rachel excused herself and her and Shane went outside to talk. She thanked and paid him for his hard work. They had a wonderful dinner with a bottle of wine while music played in the background. Now that they were both intoxicated, Rachel crawled over to him on the bed with her ass arched high in the air and the bowl of melted chocolate in her hand. She dipped her finger into the bowl and place drops of chocolate on various parts of his body, starting with his legs and working her way up. With long, sensual licks she removed the chocolate with her hot tongue sending a vibe of sweet sensation throughout his body. Through the corner of her eyes, she could see his manhood twitching anxiously as her tongue worked toward it. She then put some chocolate on his manhood and licked it off, causing him to moan and his body to shake. With on shift movement, he smacked her ass and told her to get on the black stallion and she did. They spent the night in the tent, enjoying each other, and for the second time they didn't use any protection.

The next morning, they went back to their room, packed; and then spent the day in bad watching their homemade porno. Rachel loved seeing herself on the screen; it turned her on even more than making it.

"Oh babes you look like a professional, we should do this more often. Are you sure you've never done this before?" Omar said.

"You are the first but then again you do bring out my wild side. But you know that we are going to have to destroy it before we leave?"

"What you don't trust me?"

"It's not about trusting you; I don't want to end up like Tommy Lee and Pamela Anderson with my business all exposed."

"Okay, but can we watch it again?"

"Only if you give me some more of what I like before we leave."

"Your wish is my command." After granting her wish a few times, they took a shower together. Once they were done they hardly had time to get ready before Shane buzzed and told them their cab had arrived; with suitcases in tow they left for the airport.

CHAPTER TWENTY-EIGHT

TRACY ARRIVED AT seven fifty-five and Vanessa welcomed her in. As they both looked at each other's stomachs, Tracy then handed her the cheese cake and entered into the house. Vanessa showed her to the living room, where Howard was.

"Would you like something to drink?"

"Yes, I'll have some milk please."

"You don't mind if we eat in the living room besides keeping an eye on Howard, the Chicago Bulls are playing and I'm not one to miss a game."

"No, that's not a problem; I'm not one to miss a game either."

Vanessa went into the kitchen, poured two glasses of milk: put the milk, the containers of Chinese food, alone with Howard's medicine on a tray and went back into the living room. When she arrived she saw Tracy sitting on the floor beside Howard with his hand in hers. Vanessa's heart clenched with anger, but she knew it wasn't the time or place to react. Instead, she put on a fake smile and then placed the tray on the living room table.

"It's time to take your medicine, honey."

Even though Howard knew that he needed the medication, he hated taking it because it made him feel worse. It was weird having both Vanessa and Tracy in the same room. Trying to be nice to each other because of him but he could also feel the tension between them. When Tracy saw that she was in the way, she moved onto the couch. Although he was at home, he was still hooked up to a machine because he wasn't able to eat on his own. Vanessa measured the medicine and put it into the machine. She then gave him the other medication by mouth. At this point, he was so debilitated that he could hardly sit up to take the medicine, so she held the back of his head.

"You don't mind if we watch the basketball game while we eat?" Vanessa asked him.

"No, go ahead. The medication knocks me out, so you two won't be bothering me at all." he replied.

"Is there anything else you need?"

"Yes. Just one more thing; come over here please." She walked over and sat down beside him. He looked into her eyes and said,

"I don't want you to ever forget that I will always love you and anything that I've ever done to hurt you wasn't done intentionally. I was being selfish and inconsiderate especially after I found out I had cancer. Now give me a kiss so you can watch the game." She gave him a long, meaningful kiss that made his manhood rise. It was just a shame he couldn't put it to good use. His body was so weak that the only thing he could do was return the kiss.

Although, Howard was partially on his dying bed, Tracy wished that she was Vanessa. She always knew that Howard would never love her the way she wanted him too and now seeing how much he loved his wife caused great pain to her heart. She wondered how she had even gotten herself into this situation in the first place. When she had seen Howard again years ago she knew he was married but that didn't stop her from wanting him. She knew that he only wanted to have sex with her so she settled for the little bit of nothing that he was offering her. Never once did she think about Vanessa, it was always about what she wanted.

Even now on his dying bed she still ended up with nothing. However, just being able to be here with him eased her pain. She would always have a part of him once the baby was born. She only hoped that Vanessa's resentment against her would not stop their kids from being a part of each other's lives.

After a quiet dinner, Vanessa and Tracy went into the kitchen and had cheese cake and decaffeinated coffee. At this point, Vanessa knew it was time to question her about her husband.

"So, when are you due?" she asked.

"In about eight weeks. And you?"

"Actually, I'm also due in eight week. My husband seemed to be quite busy that month." Unable to find the right words to say, Tracy thought it would be best not to say anything.

"If you don't mind me asking how long have you known my husband?"

"I met him right after he left home; we lived together while he was in school. Our relationship was very intense but it ended when he was in his second year of college. Years later we would meet up after work at Rick's Pub." Tracy didn't want to get Howard into any trouble but at the same time she felt Vanessa deserved to know the truth. Plus she wanted Vanessa to know that although he loved his wife he was once in love with her.

"I knew it!" Vanessa said.

"Knew what?" asked Tracy.

"That was just after I had the twins, and we fought over just about everything. Every day he would come home from work, have dinner and spend some time with the girls and me. He would then give the girls a bath, put them to bed and leave; some nights he wouldn't even come home. As much as he loved the girls, he really wanted a boy and for that reason as well as others our relationship went downhill. For one whole year after the girls were born, we hardly had sex, so I knew he was getting it from someone else."

Tracy could see the tears in Vanessa's eyes but there was nothing she could honestly say at that point to prevent them from falling.

"When I did see him years later he told me that he was married and that he had twin girls. All he would do is talk about you and the kids because he wanted his marriage to work. It was hard for me to hear about you because I had just come out of a bad relationship. I was jealous of you because all he talked about was you and it made me sick to hear your name. It got to the point where both of us were depending on each other's comfort. So, when the subject changed to how long it had been since either of us had had sex we both realized that we both were in need. A month after that conversation we were sleeping together again and soon your name wasn't being mention at all. However, it was two years after I found out that he was married that we started sleeping together again."

"So, that's supposed to make me feel better because you waited. How about the fact that he was married, didn't that cross your mind?" Tracy could see that the conversation was heading in a direction that she didn't feel comfortable with and she felt that the more she explained the deeper she dug herself in.

"Can you please just answer the question?" Vanessa said.

"When you moved into the house, he told me that he didn't want to see me anymore because he needed to concentrate on his family."

"Did he ever buy you anything or take you anywhere?"

"Years ago when we lived together yes he would buy me things but not after he was married. The only thing he ever bought me was food or drinks and we never went anywhere. We didn't even go to my place. The only place we would ever have sex was in the back room of Rick's Pub." The more Tracy talked, the more she realized how cheap and dirty the nothingness that she shared with Howard was.

"After we broke up and because of the reason we broke up he didn't have much respect for me. He always made sure that I was aware of how much he loved his family and that I should never expect anything more than what he was already giving me, which was just sex. However, for some sick reason I couldn't stop loving him and he knew it. That's when he decided to call it quits. We both lost contact with each other and I went on with my life, even though I never forgot about him. Then eight months ago, I got a big promotion and my girls took me out for drinks to celebrate. I decided that because Howard was the one who had encouraged me to go back to school and pursue my career; that I would go back to the place where I last seen him. It was just a coincidence that he happened to be there that night.

We talked about old times, I drank more that I could handle, and before I knew it we were doing it in the back of the bar. It wasn't something we planned, it just happened. I'm not sure, but I think he was waiting for you that night."

"How do you know that?" Vanessa asked.

"Because that night I came back, hoping to find him, but when I did, he was sitting in the far back booth with a lady. I didn't get to see her face because I didn't want him to see me."

As hard as it was to hear the truth it had to be said. Vanessa knew that once Howard was gone she wanted Tracy's child to be a part of their lives so, that the kids would be a part of each other's lives. Although Vanessa blamed Howard she didn't want to spend the rest of his life being mad at him and it made no sense to be mad at Tracy.

Vanessa felt like she was on the verge of a nervous breakdown, she could feel a lump forming in her throat, and there were tears in her eyes. Not wanting to cry in front of the woman her husband had betrayed her with. She tried to hold back the tears, but they had a mind of their own. They followed down her cheeks into her mouth, tasting like salt. Her heart ached and her mind was confused with anger, but yet she couldn't express her feeling to her husband and she wasn't about to express them to her husband's mistress; she needed her sister.

Vanessa and Tracy sat talking for hours, telling each other all sorts of things as if they were old friends. They even touched each other's stomach and felt the babies move. It was a time of bonding for both of them and Vanessa knew that it was what Howard wanted. Vanessa also understood why he wanted them to be friends because he wanted his girls to know their brother or sister. Tracy spent that night and the next couple of day with Vanessa and Howard; it was as if they were one big happy family.

As much as Vanessa didn't want to get along with the woman who had helped caused her so much pain, it was hard not to like her. After all there was nothing wrong with her besides the fact that she was pregnant by her husband. That week they went shopping for baby clothes and when they got back, the three of them talked for hours until Howard fell asleep. Vanessa was so shocked to see that Howard was even able to stay up so long but at the same time, she was glad.

CHAPTER TWENTY-NINE

LORRAINE WAS AWOKEN by something poking her in her lower back. Steveroy had slept over and there was no doubt what he was in the mood for. His manhood was rock hard as he continued to poke her; it wasn't until he said "I'm hungry" that she turned around.

"And what exactly are you hungry for?"

"How about I show you?"

He eased himself under the covers and found his way to her pot of gold. Lorraine was amazed at how long he stayed under there without suffocating. He had her eyes rolling in the back of her head from pleasure and within minutes her juices were flowing. Once he emerged from under the covers he told her to get in his favorite position, at the edge of the bed with her ass arched high in the air. Lorraine didn't have to be told twice as she positioned herself. She loved the way he made love to her, by making sure she was satisfied every time. After they took a shower Steveroy went into the kitchen to make breakfast. While watching him preparing breakfast Lorraine decided to call Vanessa. On the second ring, somebody picked up the phone, but she didn't recognize the voice.

"Can I speak with Vanessa please?"

"Yes hold on please?" Tracy replied.

"Hello"

"Vanessa, its Lorraine. Who the hell was that?"

"It's a long story."

"I got the time."

"Well, if you really must know, I guess I'll just have to tell you, but just as long as you don't put your two cents in."

"Is it that bad?" Lorraine said.

"You'll see for yourself."

"Wait before we get into all of that, how is Howard doing?"

"Well as good as expected but I'm having a hard time with it. The doctor told me that the girls need to spend as much time with him because they don't know how much time he has left. I have taken, so many days off from work just to be by his side. As much as I miss the girls they are only going to add more stress to my life and I still haven't heard from Rachel, so she has no idea about anything that's going on".

Vanessa spoke one run-on sentence after the next. Before Vanessa could continue Lorraine asked her if she wanted to have lunch with her, because she could tell Vanessa needed to get out of the house and just take a break from it all.

"That is actually a good idea; I would love that, how about we make it a late lunch." Vanessa said.

"What time is good for you?"

"Say two o'clock at the Zen Garden."

"Sounds good, see you then and don't think I'm going to forget to question you about whoever that was that answered the phone. See you soon bye." replied Lorraine.

"Bye"

Lorraine turned her attention back to the handsome but young man that was making her breakfast, half naked in her kitchen.

"You don't mind if I go for lunch with Vanessa do you?"

"No, that's fine with me."

"Are you going to stay here or go into the office?"

"If it's okay with you, I'll stay here."

"That's exactly what I wanted to hear."

After breakfast they went back to bed and relaxed unit it was time for Lorraine to leave. Four hours later Lorraine was making her way to the Zen Garden in Steveroy's new BMW X5. He had insisted that she drive his car because he needed her to know that she was a part of his life and he wanted to share everything with her. As she drove she couldn't help but feeling like she was falling in love. Steveroy was everything she had been looking for and although she was eleven years older than him it no longer mattered because she knew he genuinely cared and wanted to be with her. He attended to her every need and loved to hear about her day. He was just everything that she needed him to be. It had been years since she was in a serious relationship and it really help that he was well educated, so that he could keep up with his end of a conversation. She pulled into the Zen Garden parking lot and looked for a spot.

CHAPTER THIRTY

TYRONE WAS TALKING on the sex line with his manhood in his hand, pleasuring himself when Vanessa knocked on the door. She asked him to listen out for Howard's nurse because she was going out for lunch and then she was picking up the twins from Ms. Bedford. As soon as he knew she was out of the house he checked on Howard, who was fast asleep and then called his ex Michelle to come over. Although, he knew that she was only coming for the money and the drugs, it was nice to have her around. Many times he wanted to talk to her about the robbery but he knew he couldn't. She was not one to keep a secret; especially when she could get paid to keep her mouth shut. Michelle was the love of his life; they had an on again off again relationship that lasted for seven years.

Five years into their relationship it became very toxic and just when Tyrone decided to leave her she told him she was pregnant. Being pregnant just made Michelle even more demanding and she constantly found reasons to fight with him about any and everything. Michelle was six months pregnant when they got into a very heated argument. She hit him several times before he decided it would be best that he leave the house. Instead of just allowing him to leave she followed him outside and begged him to stay. Filled with anger and rage she followed him and three blocks from their house she wrapped her car around a tree. Unaware of the accident Tyrone spent the night at Leroy's house and two days later Michelle's sister informed him that she was in an accident. After losing the baby, spending a month in the hospital and six months in rehab Michelle and Tyrone agreed it would be best they go their separate ways.

However Michelle never really recovered from her accident and the loss of her baby. She became very dependent on the medication that she needed to take for her day to day pain. Losing her baby devastated her especially when she found out that it was very unlikely that she could ever get pregnant again. She then turned to street drugs when her doctor wouldn't give her as much medication as she needed. It became clear to Dr. Flanagan that she was becoming dependent on her medication. Four years later Michelle was still on drugs, wasn't working and was living with her mother.

Although their relationship ended years ago they still remain friends and would hook up once in awhile; so when Tyrone asked her to come over she was excited. Michelle wasn't one of those crack heads that looked like a crack head she took very good care of herself and from the outside it seemed like she had the drugs under control but it was destroying her on the inside.

After making something to eat Tyrone went back into his room and opened his last bottle of rum; he needed it to take the edge off. By the time Michelle rang the door bell he was half way finished the bottle and needed something to smoke. Before allowing her to come in they both had a cigarette; while rolling a joint on the front porch. They sat talking and smoking the joint until the nurse came; once done they went inside and before going into his room Tyrone checked on Howard; who was still sleeping. By the time he got into his room Michelle was lining up the coke on his night stand. She was in her early forties with no kids, very athletic body and firm breast. She really knew how to treat a man sexually as she removed his pants and told him to sit down. After he finished his lines Michelle got on her knees and pulled his manhood out of his shorts. Licking the tip first she then slowly worked her tongue up and down the length of his shaft while holding him at the base. She continued working her magic on him as he became hard inside her mouth and released in her mouth. Tyrone was amazed at how well she was able to swallow as if it was something she did all the time but then again it probably was because of the type of lifestyle she lived. Tyrone then told her to take her clothes off and dance for him and she did as she was told. Throughout the night Tyrone continued to tell her what he wanted, how he wanted it and she was the obedient child because she knew, she would be paid well.

CHAPTER THIRTY-ONE

ON HER WAY to meet Lorraine, Vanessa called Ms. Bedford to let her know that she would be picking up the girls after five. Ms. Bedford informed her that it would not be a problem. She then asked about Howard's condition and filled Vanessa in on the girl's behavior, and then hung up the phone.

As she entered the Zen Garden Vanessa looked around for Lorraine and spotted her in the far corner. It was nice to be out of the house, away from Howard and the kids because with everything that was going on in her life she needed the break. Lorraine didn't even see Vanessa approach the table because she was lost in her thoughts about Steveroy. She couldn't help but feel like she was dreaming; he had turned out to be more than she could ever imagine he would be. Vanessa had to call her twice before she got her attention.

"Hey girl where's your mind at?"

"Oh sorry, honestly I was thinking about Steveroy. That man has got me twisted." Lorraine got up and gave Vanessa a big hug before she allowed her to sit down.

"Well I don't blame you. You have yourself a fine young black man that loves you and can financially take care of you."

"How do you know that he loves me?"

"Oh yeah I forgot to tell you, the night of the party we were talking and he told me. He said that he was done with these young girls who didn't know what they wanted and had some crazy baby daddy that they were still sleeping with in hopes of getting him back."

"What, so why didn't you tell me?"

"I'm sorry with everything going on with Howard it slipped my mind but girl that man loves you."

Lorraine couldn't contain her smile because deep in her heart she felt the same way but was scared of getting hurt again. Not wanting to think about her feelings for Steveroy Lorraine changed the subject.

"So how is Howard doing?"

"Honestly like I was saying earlier he isn't doing very well and I really don't know how much time he has to live."

"Oh Vanessa I'm so sorry. Is there anything I can do?"

"Right now there isn't much anyone can do but enjoy the time he has left. I feel like I'm being pulled in so many directions. I'm so glad that you and Kim are around but I still can't get a hold of my sister, and then I'm also dealing with Tracy."

"Has Rachel contacted you as of yet?"

"No!"

"So you have no idea where she is?"

"All I do know is that she is somewhere with Omar". It's not like she has to tell me everywhere she goes but it's almost a week since I've heard from her; the least she could do is give me a call to let me know she is okay."

"I am surprised that she hasn't called you; but who the hell is this Tracy chick? Is she the one that answered the phone?" At this point the waiter placed their order on the table, Vanessa waited for her to leave before answering Lorraine's question.

"Yes she is. "Now Lorraine I only want you to listen, I know you can be very opinionated, so please I need you to understand why I'm putting up with this in the first place."

"Okay, I'll try to keep my opinion to myself."

"Thanks. Tracy is the other women; Howard was cheating on me with. It's been going on for over two years but apparently he did break it off with her last year. However once he found out that he had cancer he started to sleep around again. Now if you think that's bad she is also pregnant and to top it off she is due the same time as I am. I actually had dinner with her last night and I realized that beside that fact that we are both pregnant for Howard we have a lot in common. I feel like such a fool, how could I not have known that my husband was cheating on me but then again I didn't even know that he was sick"

As Vanessa spoke she was unable to hold back the tears. It was really hard for her to deal with Howard's infidelity but knowing that his mistress was having his child was killing her inside. Lorraine stretched across the table and held Vanessa's hand. Not only was she about to lose her husband but she now had to live with the fact that she also wanting the twins to know their brother or sister. Having Tracy's child be a part of their lives would be a constant reminder of what Howard had done.

"None of this is your fault, so don't blame yourself Vanessa. Regardless of what Howard has done I know that he loves you and that's what you have to hold onto right now.

"Can you believe that he fucked her the same day he fucked me and we both got pregnant that night, now what are the odds in that. Never mind I now have to explain to my kids why their brothers or sisters are the same age but they have two different mothers."

Lorraine wanted to tell her to lower her voice but she didn't want to upset her any more than she already was, so she got up, sat next to her and put her arms around her. At first Vanessa was tense but shortly after she warmed up to Lorraine's hug and melted in her arms as she felt a small weight lifted off her shoulders.

CHAPTER THIRTY-TWO

WHEN RACEL AND Omar arrived at the airport it was packed. It was a good thing that they had arrived two hours early because otherwise they would have missed their flight. After what seemed like forever they were finally able to board the plane. As they boarded the plane the flight attendant told them that they could sit where ever they wanted to because the plane wasn't packed. They decided to sit near the back and Rachel sat directly across from Omar, giving him a clear view as she crossed her legs. As soon as the plane took off Omar ordered two drinks, although it was his idea for the trip he was never a big fan of flying. It usually took him three to four drinks to calm his nerves.

Rachel was wearing a knee length dress that was cut very low in the back. She could see the hunger in Omar's eyes as he licked his lips and told her to open her legs so he could stare at her sweetness. Once the flight attendants were no longer walking around Rachel took off her panties and threw them at Omar. Amazed at what she was doing as he quickly looked around to see if anyone could see them. Glad that the coast was clear he got on his knees and told her to make sure no one was coming. Finding it hard to concentrate on her task Rachel tried her best not to close her eyes and get lost in the moment as she opened her legs wider. Unable to control herself any longer she pushed him away and got up. Her dress was soaking wet as she made her way to the bathroom. While her pussy pulsates with every step she took towards the bathroom she knew that he would follow her. She went into the bathroom and seconds later Omar opened the door with a big grin on his face. He came at her like an animal ready to devour its prey. Grateful that the plane was practically empty he locked the door and savagely exposed her breast. He then backed her up against the door and manhandled her left breast as he devoured the other with his mouth.

As Rachel struggled to contain herself; Omar placed one then two fingers inside of her moist pussy; he then tasted his fingers. She could taste her sweetness on his lips as he passionately kissed her; she moaned while breathing heavily. With passion filled eyes Rachel carefully lowered herself inside the confined space and pulled his pants down. Taking his manhood into her hand she started to play with him real slowly at first and then faster as Omar begged her to put it in her mouth. Playfully she sucked the tip, then lick up and down the sides, she then deep throat his manhood and started to suck harder while going up and down his shaft. She could feel his explosion about to happen as his dick became swollen inside of her mouth. Not wanting him to explode she stood up, turned around and told him to go deep. He pushed her up against the door and forced every inch of his hardness deep within her hot awaiting pussy. A soft moan escaped Rachel's lips as she felt every inch of him enter her pleasure box. After twenty minutes of hard-core fucking, they heard someone banging on the door but Omar didn't care because he wasn't about to stop until they were both done. Five minutes later, Rachel's body began to shake like an erupting volcano and she could feel him swelling inside of her. With every bit of strength that Omar had left he picked up his speed as he released his load without protection once again inside of her.

By now the person outside was begging for them to open the door, so they got dressed and walk out of the bathroom as if nothing had just happened and went back to their seats. Instead of sitting across from each other Rachel sat beside him and they slept for the remainder of the flight.

"Honey we're home" Omar said as Rachel sat up. Although she had slept most of the five hour flight, the sexual encounter with Omar had really drained all of her energy. Rachel's body was moving slow motion as they exited the plane, Omar kept having to stop so she could catch up to him.

"Am I walking too fast or is there something wrong?" "No babes. I'm just exhausted. I can't wait to get home and get into my own bed." She replied.

Once outside of the airplane Rachel's phone was able to pick up reception. Her phone beeped and vibrated indicating that she had both messages and text. She looked at her phone and decided that she would wait until she got home and took a shower before she picked up her messages.

CHAPTER THIRTY-THREE

WHILE STILL COMFORTING Vanessa, Lorraine had to ask her why she thought it would be best that Tracy come live with them.

"Like I said, we don't know how much time he has left and now is not the time to be fighting. Plus, he did try to tell me about her a couple of months ago and I didn't want to hear it."

"What do you mean he tried? Well maybe he should have tried hard to keep his pecker in his pants, so that you wouldn't have to be dealing with all of this right now."

"Well like I said I do want the kids to know each other so, that means I have to have contact with the Tracy."

"I guess that's one way of looking at it, but how do you feel? Is this something you can handle, or are you just dealing with it because you feel you have to?"

"Okay! One question at a time girl. Yes I am just dealing with it but not because I have to but I want to. He may have done me wrong, but now is not the time to let him pay for what he has done. It's time to put all of that aside and enjoy the time we have left. Why should the kids have to suffer for their mistakes."

"You're right, and I'm sorry. Are you up for company tomorrow night? If so Steveroy and I can drop by for a BBQ we'll bring the meat?"

"Actually that would be great. I can use the company" said Vanessa.

"Okay, Steveroy and I have some things to do in the morning but we can be there around three."

Twenty minutes later Vanessa and Lorraine were giving each other hugs And kisses before going to their cars. After picking up the girls, Vanessa brought them to the mall. She wanted them to buy something special for their father. It took them almost forty-five minutes before deciding on a necklace that said number one dad inside of a heart with a diamond at the tip of the heart. She also bought the girls the same necklace but theirs said daddy's little girl. It almost cost an arm and a leg, but it was worth it.

Before going home Vanessa took the girls to Playland inside the mall and as she watched them play with the other kids, she started to cry. She remembered how she felt when she lost her parents and how hard it was to deal with not having them around. However she was blessed to have known her parents because they didn't die until after the twins were born. There was so much the girl would be missing out on once their father was gone. It scared Vanessa to think that kids would have no memories of their father because they were so young.

CHAPTER THIRTY-FOUR

RACHEL AND OMAR arrived at her apartment with only one thing on their minds: sleep. Although, Rachel had planned to check her messages; after taking a nice hot shower with Omar, they both ended up falling asleep on Rachel's bed without any clothes on. It wasn't until Omar's cell phone rang that he realized he had slept the day away. It was his right hand man, Paul, telling him he needed to come into the office to close the IMB contract. Omar told Paul that he would meet him at the office because the contract was at his place. Instead of waking Rachel up he wrote her a note and left. Omar had been dealing with Mr. Highlander for the past six months trying to convince him that going with his company was the best thing for everyone involved. Forty five minutes later Omar walked into his office to find everyone waiting for him.

To Omar's surprise, they didn't send Mr. Highlander to close the deal. Paul Introduced her as Tiffany and then left the room. Although she was an attractive black woman, his first impression of Tiffany was that she was a very flirtatious and sexual woman; by the way she looked into his eyes when she shook his hand. Tiffany was shocked to find out that she wouldn't be dealing with Paul, but Omar instead. It was so easy for her to talk Paul into doing whatever she wanted. She already had him wrapped around her finger. Oh well, she would just have to wrap Omar around her finger even tighter.

"What happened to Mr. Highlander? We had everything almost ready before I left town?"

"Mr. Highlander has been very sick. You don't have a problem dealing with me, do you?" Tiffany said.

"No."

"If so, he should be back to work in a few days and you can always wait until then."

"Like I said it won't be a problem just as long as you're up-to-date with everything Mr. Highlander and I have already discussed."

"Yes, he has explained everything to me. A few things have changed but we can go through the new contract over lunch before we sign."

When Omar looked over the contract he realized that a lot of things had changed. So, he called Rachel to let her know he would be tied up longer than he thought. After trying to reach Rachel at home, then on her cell phone and not getting a hold of her he left a message on her cell phone.

Rachel woke to find Omar not in bed; she called out thinking that he must be in the bathroom. When there was no reply, she got out of bed and went into the bathroom brushed her teeth and washed her face. She was shocked when she realized the time because of the difference time zones she had slept in which was something she never did especially considering she had gone to bed so early. She was about to go into the kitchen when noticed Omar's note by the phone. While reading the note, she pushed the button on the answering machine. After listening to three messages she heard her sister's tearful voice telling her that Howard was in the hospital and by the recording she realized that it was sent two days after they left. Without calling her sister she took a quick shower; put on a pair of track pants, a t-shirt, wrote a note for Omar and left. On her way there she remembered that she left her phone but there was no way she was going back to get it. The entire way there she prayed that Howard was okay because she would never be able to forgive herself for not being there for her sister if he wasn't. Rachel felt overwhelmed with guilt because it was unlike her not to call her sister but she was so caught up with Omar that she had failed to be there when sister needed her the most. She pulled into the driveway, ran up to the house and rang the door bell. When the door opened Rachel looked around to make sure she had the right door because she didn't recognized the person that answered the door.

"Is Vanessa there?"

"No she isn't; can I get your name and I'll let her know you stopped by."

"No you can't and who the hell are you?" Rachel said as she walked passed her. Once inside Rachel looked around until she saw Howard lying on the couch. As she approached him she realized that he was sleeping, so she turned her attention back to the person that had answered the door.

"Are you his nurse?"

"No."

"Okay then who the hell are you?"

"I'm Tracy and you are?"

"I'm Vanessa's sister, where is she and really who the hell are you?"

Tracy felt that is wasn't her place to explain to Vanessa's sister as to who she was. So, instead she told her that Vanessa would be home shortly and it would be better if she explained. She then offered to make her a cup of tea, realizing that she hadn't eaten all day Rachel accepted her offer. Although Rachel wanted to know who this pregnant woman inside her sister's house was; she did seem like a nice person and because of that they were able to have a nice conversation about other things.

CHAPTER THIRTY-FIVE

WHEN VANESSA AND the girls arrived home Rachel and Tracy were sitting on the porch. The girls ran up and hugged their aunt; they then looked over at Tracy and Tianna asked.

"Who are you?" The question came so quickly that Vanessa could hardly make out which one of the girls was asking, but it really didn't matter because they were both thinking the same thing.

"Oh you must be Tonya and Tianna. Your mom and dad have told me a lot about you two. My name is Tracy. I'm just a friend." Not a friend of mine, Vanessa thought to herself, but of course she didn't say it out load, unfortunately.

"Girls please go to your room and I'll be in, in a minute, then you can show daddy what you got for him. I know he'll love it." Vanessa suggested to the girls. She then walked over to her sister and almost melted in her arms, as an uncontrollable amount of tear poured out of her. Once she was able to regain herself, she started yelling at her sister, while telling her everything that had happened in the past week. Rachel was in shock with everything that she was hearing, there was nothing she could say to excuse the fact that she wasn't there for her so, she just listened with tears in her eyes. Not wanting to intrude Tracy walked around to the back of the house to go throw the back door.

In a more understandable voice Vanessa updated her sister on Howard's condition and who Tracy was. At that moment Rachel wanted to hate Howard for what he was putting her sister through but she just couldn't in his condition. She knew that she had to put her feeling for Howard aside and just be there for her sister. The baby, the girls and just maybe if she dug deep enough she could also be there for Tracy and her baby too. However, that would take some time.

From what her sister had told her about Tracy; she was with Howard before Vanessa met him and although she knew that Howard was now married she was still with him

"Vanessa I know you have a big heart and you have always been there for your family and friends, but do you really think that this is the right thing to do."

"I truly understand what you're saying and Lorraine has been saying the same thing but do you remember when we found out that dad had a son?"

"Of course I do; it almost ripped our family apart" Rachel said.

"Well don't you ever wonder about our brother? He's out there somewhere living a life we are not even apart of; well I don't want that to happen to my kids and they shouldn't have to suffer because of their parents."

There was nothing left for Rachel to say because she now knew and understood why her sister was doing what she was doing.

"Well now that you put it like that I truly understand and I'll be by your side every step of the way."

"So have you ever thought about our brother?" Vanessa asked.

"Where is this coming from? Here we are talking about your situation and you mention our brother."

"I've been thinking a lot about him lately because of Howard's condition and how short life can be".

"It's weird because I use to think about him all the time when we first found out but since mom and dad died; the only time I do is when I meet someone his age" Rachel said.

"Well before all this shit happened I was looking for him and I have his number."

"So why haven't you tried to call him?"

"Because I was scared I wouldn't know what to say. Can you believe he just lives in Milton?" Vanessa said.

"What that's only an hour away. We need to make that call."

"What if he doesn't want to see us?"

"Well at least we'll know that we tried" said Rachel.

"Okay let me go get the number" Vanessa said.

She went inside to find Howard awake and the girls showing him the gift they had bought him. After making sure Howard was okay she went into the kitchen to get the number. She grabbed the phone and then went back outside.

"Okay here's the number you make the call."

"Why does it have to be me?"

"Because I got the number so you call." Without agreeing with her sister Rachel took the paper and made the call. It rang several times and just as she was about to hang up; she heard a deep male voice.

"Hello." Rachel was unable to speak.

"Hello!" Dmitri repeated. Vanessa quickly took the phone from Rachel. As she put the phone to her ear she could hear the person saying hello repeatedly.

"Hello can I speak with Dmitri please?"

"This is. Who is this?"

"This is Vanessa Blackwood your sister."

Dmitri was shocked when the person on the other line said she was his sister. Although his mother had told him that his father had left them to live with his other family. He couldn't believe that she was actually calling him after all these years. Vanessa put the phone on speaker so that Rachel could hear too. They talked for an hour and arranged for him to come visit the next day.

"Now that wasn't so hard was it?" Vanessa said.

"No, but he sounds so much like daddy with that deep voice."

"I know and I can't wait to see him." Just then Tonya came outside.

"Mommy daddy wants you."

They both went into the house; once inside Vanessa gave Howard his medication and went into the kitchen to make a pot of decaffeinated coffee. Rachel stayed in the living room so that she could talk to Howard; she was able to find out more about his condition. It was hard seeing him like this because he had always been a very handsome man and so full of life but now looking at him he had lost over twenty pounds and it showed a lot in his face.

CHAPTER THIRTY-SIX

INSTEAD OF GOING into the guest room Tracy decided to go into the back yard but was shocked to see a half naked man lying on the lawn chair. Vanessa had told her that one of Howard's friends was staying with them but she had never actually seen him while she was there. When Tyrone heard the noise from her shoes he opened his eyes and immediately recognized that is was Tracy; however he laid there stoned out of his mind unable to move to cover himself.

"Your name is Tracy right?"

"Yes and you are?"

"I'm Tyrone."

"Oh, Vanessa told me one of Howard's friends was staying here. It's nice to meet you."

"So you don't remember meeting me before?"

"No."

"Well let me refresh your memory."

Tracy looked him over to see if she could remember who he was but she couldn't. With a devilish look on his face he explained where they had met.

"One night at Rick's Pub you were drunk out of your mind. I watched you go into the back room with Howard. I could only guess but after Howard finish fucking your brains out; you came out crying. You looked around for Howard but he had left. I was sitting at the bar and you came over and asked me to buy you a drink. I tried to convince you that you didn't need another drink but you insisted, so I gave you another one. We got to talking and you started to come onto me and the next thing I knew I was fucking your brains out in the back room."

As he spoke it was all starting to come back to her. It was the night Howard told her that he didn't need her services any more. She had begged him to tell her why but instead he told her that if she gave him oral sex he would. So, she did and instead of explaining he ejaculated in her mouth and left the room. Although, Tracy had wanted to forget about that night and she almost did; she had no idea that Tyrone was one of Howard's friends the night they slept together. Now here he was reminding her of something she had tried so hard to forget. She was about to turn and walk back to the front of the house but he asked her to stay. She really didn't want to stay there with him; she also didn't want him to know that she was ashamed of what he had just told her. So she sat down in the lawn chair across from him.

"So what are you doing here?" he asked.

"It's a long story and I'm sure you'll hear about it soon enough." she said.

"Fine don't tell me." Tyrone tried to make small talk with her but she wasn't in the mood to talk, so he gave up, lay back down and closed his eyes. Shortly after Tracy walked back to the front of the house and was glad that Vanessa and her sister had gone inside. When she walked into the house everyone was in the living room with Howard so she went into the kitchen to get a drink.

"Tracy there is a plate in the microwave for you." Vanessa yelled out.

"Okay thank you." It really warmed Tracy's heart to see how much Vanessa was trying to make her feel welcomed under the circumstances. She set the microwave for a minute and then sat at the table to eat, when she was done she washed the dishes and went upstairs to the spare room; where she had been sleeping. It was still early so she checked her answering machine and returned some calls. Grateful that she was able to do most of her work from home she decided to fire up her computer and returned some e-mails. After going through most of her e-mails she came across one that caught her attention; it was from one of her biggest clients Mr. Santana. His e-mail stated that he was coming into town in a week but it was sent five days ago which meant she only had two days to prepare; so she called her receptionist.

"Hi Antoinette, are you aware that Mr. Santana is coming into town in two day?"

"Hi Tracy, yes and I was just about to call you because when I was working on his file the computer crashed. I lost all the work you did as well as the work I did." By the tone of Antoinette's voice Tracy could tell she was panicking.

"Don't worry I have a copy of what I have done on my computer, I'll come in tomorrow and we can work on it together. Arrange for someone to cover the front desk for the morning."

"Thank God, I'll get Janelle to cover me and I will see you in the morning." They said bye and ended the call. As soon as Antoinette was off the phone she arranged a surprise baby shower for Tracy. She collected money from everyone in the office and along with two other girls they went shopping. They managed to get all the decorations: ordered a cake, food and drink, baby clothes, gift baskets and five gift cards from different store worth two hundred and fifty each.

Tracy returned the rest of her e-mails and by nine-thirty she was so exhausted she went to bed.

The next morning Tracy got dressed, went back to her apartment and did two loads of laundry before going into the office. When she arrived the office was buzzing with excitement as everyone shouted surprise. Tracy was overwhelmed by the amount of gifts and food that was there but mostly because they actually cared enough to do all of this just for her. There were baby shower games, someone walking around with a video camera, someone taking pictures and a book for everyone to sign their name.

Three hours later a few of the guys were loading everything into her car by the time they were done the only space that was available was the driver's seat. As she drove back to her apartment she wondered how the hell she was going to bring everything upstairs. After she parked the car she grabbed everything on the passenger seat and went into the building. Once upstairs she went through all the bags with pure excitement when she saw all the cute baby clothes she got. Everything was either green or yellow because they weren't sure if she was having a boy or girl. Just then she could hear her neighbour's kids in the hallway so she decided to ask them if they could help her bring the rest of things upstairs. After unpacking everything she thought her living room looked like an unkempt toy store. By the time she was finished cleaning her apartment she was too tired to drive back to Howard and Vanessa's place; so she spent the night and left in the morning.

CHAPTER THIRTY-SEVEN

TIFFANY WAS USED to getting what she wanted especially when it came to men but her advances were getting on Omar's last nerve. Although he had told her that he was in a committed relationship she continued to hit on him. As much as he wanted Mr. Highlander to sign on with the company he wasn't about to jeopardize his relationship just to get him to sign.

"Look I've told you I'm in a relationship and if you continue to make passes at me we are going to have to end this meeting now!"

Shocked and embarrassed that he was actually turning her down Tiffany agreed. After Omar's outburst it was very uncomfortable for them to go on, so he left Paul in charge and went back to Rachel's place. They had ordered Red Lobster for lunch but he hadn't eaten so he packed it up for Rachel. It was after nine by the time Omar got to Rachel's only to realize that she wasn't home. Glad that he had a key he tried calling her on her cell but he could hear it ringing in the bedroom. He walked into the bedroom and as he was undressing he saw the note by the phone, so he redressed and left. When he arrived at Vanessa's one of the twins answered the door but he couldn't tell which one it was.

"Hi uncle Omar come in everyone is in the living room with daddy" Tianna said. As he entered the house Tianna ran into the living room yelling uncle Omar's here. While Tracy and Tyrone stayed out of sight Rachel, Vanessa, Howard and Omar talked while the girls watched a movie in the other room. Once the movie was done they wanted to see what the adults were doing, so they went into the other room. Throughout the rest of the evening the kids entertained them by singing and dancing to their favorite songs. By eleven-thirty Howard was exhausted, they had been talking so long Vanessa didn't even realize the time. It was so good to see him smiling again but she could tell that he was getting tired. Without Vanessa having to say it Rachel and Omar knew it was time for them to leave so that Howard could rest. Vanessa invited them over to the BBQ since Lorraine and Steveroy were already coming, she would also let Kim and Richard know about it as well.

Thankful that the girls were tired too she told them to say good night and go get ready for bed. She said good night to her sister and Omar locked the door and went into the kitchen to get Howard his medicine. She sat with her head on his chest as they prayed for him to get better, she the kissed him good night and went upstairs. Vanessa went into the girl's room to say good night but they weren't in their beds instead they were in her bed.

"Mommy can we please sleep with you tonight?" Tonya said.

Even though she wanted to be alone there was no way she could say no to them.

Since they had both taken their own cars Omar followed behind Rachel. As soon as they arrived back at Rachel's apartment and the door was closed Omar took her in his arms.

"Babes you know how much I love you right?"

"Yes why?" He led her into the living room and told her he would be right back. Shortly after he returned with something in his hand but she couldn't see what it was. He slipped the box into his pocket and took both of her hands in his.

"Well seeing Howard tonight made me realized that life is too short and I want to spend the rest of my life with you. Now I know that there is a lot going on right now but I love you and need you in my life. He took the box out of his pocket and opened it.

"Rachel Phillips will you marry me?" Rachel was ecstatic as she looked into his eyes not knowing that she was carrying his child and said yes.

"There has been no other man that I've ever loved more then you and my life wouldn't be complete if you weren't a part of it."

They embraced as he picked her up and carried her into the room. As he bathed her with kisses she couldn't take her eyes off of the ring; even when he was making love to her.

CHAPTER THIRTY-EIGHT

ALTHOUGH, SHE DIDN'T want to believe it Mrs. Anderson couldn't help feeling like there was something Tyrone wasn't telling her. She felt that he was somehow involved in the death of her son and finding out that he had been arrested confirmed her suspicions. It was posted in the morning paper that the police had arrested Tyrone Davis as a person of interest for the robbery and death of three men. She knew he was out on bail but wasn't able to get a hold of him on his cell phone or home number so, she call Howard.

"Good morning Vanessa its Mrs. Anderson how are you doing today?"

"I'm good Mrs. Anderson, it's nice to hear your voice and how are you doing?"

"Well you know it could be better. There isn't a day that goes by that I don't think about Leroy. Did you know he was my only son?"

"Yes I did."

"Well the reason I called is because I wanted to know if Howard knew where Tyrone is; I need to talk to him."

"He's actually here with us, hold on and I'll get him for you."

"Okay I'll hold."

Vanessa put the phone on hold and yelled out to Tyrone that Mrs. Anderson was on the phone for him. Tyrone knew that it was just a matter of time before Mrs. Anderson found out that he was staying with Howard but he still wasn't ready to except her call. He ran out of the den and told Vanessa to let her know that he wasn't home. Although, she questioned it Vanessa relayed the message and hung up with Mrs. Anderson.

"What was that all about?"

"I'm not in the mood to talk to anyone right now."

"But Mrs. Anderson, she isn't just anyone. She has been like a mother to you and she is concerned about you."

With a stern voice Tyrone said "I know but like I said I'm not in the mood so, just leave it alone Vanessa."

At that precise moment Howard walked into the kitchen and as weak as he was he looked at Tyrone and said.

"Wait a minute Tyrone don't you dare talk to my wife like that. We have done nothing but help you and if you can't respect my wife or myself while you're here then just let me know because I'll have no problem contacting your probation officer."

Without saying another word Tyrone walked out of the kitchen and went back into the den. He was glad that there was a television, a phone and a bathroom in the room; so he had no reason to leave unless he was hungry. Tyrone stayed in the room for the remainder of week, only coming out when he wanted something to eat. Mrs. Anderson had called several times after and he still refused to take her call. He only hoped that she wouldn't pop in to see him like she did at his place. Tyrone had lots to think about while he was hibernating in the room; he was to appear in court in two days and with Mrs. Anderson in the room he knew it would be even harder for him to lie to the judge. He now wished that he had listened to Howard when he had told him not to spend the money so carelessly. He had no one to talk to because his friendship with Howard was deteriorating and Leroy was gone however he had no one to blame but himself. It was just a matter of time before Mrs. Anderson would know that he was involved in the death of her son. He feared her more then he feared going to jail because she was there for him when he needed her the most which was when his mother died.

CHAPTER THIRTY-NINE

SINCE RETURNING FROM Jamaica with Richard, Kim could not be any happier because Richard had filed for a divorce and they were now living together. It was her first time living with a man and so far she was enjoying having him around. There was still a lot about Richard that she didn't know but the more she found out about him the stronger their relationship became.

Richard had stayed married way too long; for all the wrong reason and that's why it was easy for him to leave once he realized that he loved Kim. The hardest part of his divorce was leaving his son. He had a great relationship with him and at eleven he still wasn't old enough to except the fact that his parents no longer loved each other. Even though his son had met Kim many times in the past; Richard had always told him that she was just a friend from work and his son had no reason not to believe his father.

Richard was not only helping Kim with the bills he even suggested that they move into a three bedroom apartment. She agreed that he could move in and they would move into a three bedroom at the end of her lease in two months. Richard felt that Kim's two bedroom apartment wasn't big enough because she was already using the other room as an office. He needed a room so his son could visit as well he also liked to work from home.

Since living together Richard had introduced her to his co-workers and a few of his friends and tonight they were going to The Jazz Bar. One of his closes friend was playing there and he insisted that she accompanied him. When Richard arrived home from work Kim was in the shower. As he walked into the apartment he felt happy; Kim was the opposite of his soon to be ex-wife. Jenny was five years older than he was and very set in her ways. She worked part-time so that she would be home for their son but after being married to him for fourteen years she still didn't know how important it was to him that his house was kept clean. He didn't consider himself as being anal although Kim had told him he was; he just liked everything to be clean, neat and in its place. He knocked on the bathroom door before entering to find Kim with one leg on the edge of the bathtub as she shaved her legs.

"Looks like I picked the perfect time to come home. How was your day babes?"

"My day was great, hired two more girls to work the night shift and the contractor will be able to extend the bathroom at the office in one week. So I asked the guy next door if we could use his bathroom in the meantime and he said yes just as long as we use the back entrance."

"Well that sounds great. Does this mean you'll be home for your man more often?"

"Yes honey that means I will be home and your dinner will be cooked by the time you get home." As Kim continued to shave her legs Richard stripped off his clothes and got into the shower with her.

"What do you think you are doing?"

"I want to shave your pussy babes".

Excitement rushed through Kim's body as she looked up at him with a smile on her face. He then kissed her passionately and told her to sit on the edge of the tub with her legs open. Grateful that her tub wasn't the average size Kim was able to sit comfortably on the edge with both legs up along the sides. Richard got on his knees and positioned himself in front of her; using his tongue in a circular motion he worked his way up her inner thigh.

Once he reached his destination he slipped his tongue inside her sweetness and she moaned. He continued more aggressively; while holding onto both of her legs to prevent her from moving. Their voices mingled into one as their moans ricocheted throughout the bathroom; when he put one then two fingers inside her tight but sweet pussy. Unable to control her sexual excitement as every muscle in her body became taut; with one hand she grabbed onto the railing as the other took hold of his hair. With an uncontrollable desire she released her load into his mouth. With her pussy lips swollen he picked up the shaver and shaved all the hair between and on top. He then turned on the tap filled his mouth with water and sprayed the water from his mouth onto her pussy; which he repeated several times. His actions aroused her as he tightened his grip around her ankles and savagely devoured her clean shaved pussy.

He then stopped abruptly got up and took a shower; leaving her to recover on her own. She was on the verge of eruption as every nerve ending in her body ached and screamed for more. Richard was the only man that ever had this kind of power over her. With one simple touch he could control her body and his voice kept her weak whenever he spoke. The love she had for him was so intoxicating that it consumed her as she watched him washing the soap off of his body but was unable to move. Before leaving the shower he helped her up and told her to hurry up because they were now in a rush to get to The Jazz Bar.

Once she was done she wrapped a towel around herself and went into the bedroom and there on her king size bed was a box with a bow.

"What is this?"

"Why don't you open it and see."

Eagerly she went over to the bed removed the bow and opened it; not caring that the towel fell to the ground she picked up the dress. As she wiggled her way into the short sexy black and red dress she noticed that there was a card inside the box that read.

"At some point during the night I'm going to want to taste you inside The Jazz Bar so don't wear any panties." When she looked over at him he was completely dressed with a big smile on his face. She then asked him to zip her up so she could go into the bathroom to do her hair and makeup.

Twenty minutes later they were heading through the door as Richard held her hand and lead the way. The drive to the bar was exhilarating as the words on the card kept replaying in her head she reached over and removed his manhood from his pants. She then guided his penis to her lips and teased him with a couple of kisses before she took the full length of his swollen member into her mouth. He moaned and she told him to concentrate on the road as she continued to pleasure him. Unable to control himself Richard pulled over but then she stopped and told him it's just no fun when you're not driving babes. As his body craved for more he started driving again but the moment was lost and she sat back in her chair and pleasured herself. As he tried to keep his eyes on the road he couldn't resist looking at her in action every so often.

When they arrived at the bar it was packed and all Kim could think about was where they were going to go so he could pleasure her. They made their way around The Jazz Bar as Richard introduced her to his friends and then went to the bar and ordered drinks. After several drinks there was finally a booth available near the back; as they made their way over Kim could feel the moistness between her legs with every step she made. They listened to the soulful sound of his friend Peter playing the saxophone it aroused Richard so he ordered wings to distract his wicked thoughts.

"Did I tell you how beautiful you look in that dress?"

"Yes you have many times my love."

"Just being here with you makes me happy I never thought I would have the courage to leave my wife but I'm glad I did and all I can think about is moving forward with you."

Without finishing his sentence he went under the table lifted her leg and stuck his index finger inside her wet pussy. Kim looked around in shock to see if anyone could see them but once she felt his lips on her treasure box she rested her head on the booth and closed her eyes. As her nipples tingled from the sweet sensation of his lips Kim's thoughts were interrupted when the waiter came with their wings. Startled by his voice she opened her eyes to see the waiter standing there with a smile on his face as he place the platter on the table and walked away. Richard on the other hand was not fazed as he continued on his mission to make her come. It was hard for Kim to contain herself as he continued to pleasure her under the table using his fingers and tongue as she stifled her moans so no one would hear her. Kim was grateful for the loud music because when her body exploded she felt like she was going to melt and slide under the table from the heat that invaded her body. Shortly after Richard emerged from under the table with a smile on his face but wanted to hide when he noticed the waiter at the table beside them looking at him. Kim couldn't help but laugh as she watched the waiter walk away with a disgusted look on his face.

They ate the wings which were cold and ordered more drinks as they enjoyed the music. Their night ended with a big bang as they made love: in the parking lot, before leaving the car, in the elevator and several times once inside the apartment. Richard knew that when he clasped from exhaustion that he was no longer just fucking Kim he was now making love to her because all he wanted to do was hold her in his arms and fall asleep. Their relationship had come a long way in such a short time and Richard was happier than he had been in years; the only down fall was that he didn't get to see his son as often as he used to.

CHAPTER FORTY

TYRONE AWOKE SEVERAL times during the night, unable to sleep because he had court the next day. By six thirty it was senseless to even try to get some sleep, so he went to take a shower. While in the shower he thought back to the day he came up with the idea to rub Mr. Edward and now he wished that Howard or Leroy had talked him out of it.

Today was the day he would be finding out how much time he would be spending in jail. Tyrone wasn't going to be charged for Leroy death but he wasn't sure whether or not he would be found guilty for Mr. Edwards and the body guard's death that was up to the jury. He hated the fact that he had to take the rap by himself but there was no other way. Leroy was dead and Howard was on his death bed and there was no way he was going give the police Howard's name. Plus although Howard was there he didn't kill anyone. After getting out of the shower he laid on the bed with the towel wrapped around him and prayed that Leroy's mother could forgive him.

Mrs. Anderson had stopped by a week ago and he confessed to her that he was there when Leroy died. He then offered to give her the rest of the money but instead of accepting his offer she had slapped him so hard that she busted his lower lip. His lip was so bad that he should've gone to the doctor to get stitches but he didn't because he felt that he had gotten exactly what he deserved. A day later his lawyer told him that Mrs. Anderson would be testifying against him.

Tyrone was glad that Michelle had come over last night and satisfied his sexual needs because there was no way he would be taking it up the ass if today was his last day of freedom. After getting dressed he went into the kitchen to get something to eat, considering this could be his last meal before going to jail. He made a meal fit for a king and savour every bite.

Before leaving for court he wrote three letters one to Howard, one to Vanessa and the last one which was the hardest to Mrs. Anderson. He knew that most likely he would not be seeing Howard again and he wanted him to know how much his friendship had meant to him but at the same time he had to be very careful not to write anything incriminating. His letter to Vanessa explained to her how much Howard really loved her and although he made some bad choices his love for her had remained the same. He also told her that he was sorry he couldn't be there to help her raise the kids. His letter to Mrs. Anderson was straight forward, letting her know how sorry he was that Leroy was gone and that it was his idea to rob Mr. Edwards; also that he would live with the guilt forever. He even let her know that he had killed Mr. Edwards and the body guard out of anger and revenge after Mr. Edwards shot Leroy. Once done he grabbed a cab and headed to court.

Tyrone was scared but he knew that he deserved whatever happened in court. Mrs. Anderson on the other hand was a nervous wreck because she knew she would have to hear everything that had happened the night her son died. It was going to be hard because she would have to listen to Tyrone explain his involvement. What scared Mrs. Anderson the most was having to go on the witness stand and talk about her son.

As she waited for her daughter to come and pick her up she went into Leroy's old room. It had been years since Leroy lived at home but she was glad she had kept his room the same way as he had left it. She walked around the room looking at his basketball trophy and reminisced on how much he loved to play. She then looked over at his wall filled with pictures of his family and friends. Her heart nearly melted when she saw the picture of him and her at his graduation. That was one of the happiest days of his life because after dropping out of school it took him three years to realize how important it was to get an education.

Tyrone arrived at the court house with sweaty palms and butterflies in his stomach. There were reporters everywhere covering the story; pushing their mikes in his face and asking him one question after another.

"Mr. Davis do you think you'll be found guilty?"

"Mr. Davis did you murder Mr. Anderson too?"

"Mr. Davis the police reports states that Mr. Anderson could have lived if you would have called 911?"

The questions come at him from left, right and centre and as much as he wanted to answer some of them, he knew better because his words would only be twisted and used against him. Since the reporters wouldn't leave him alone he decided to wait inside the courtroom until his lawyer arrived; however he was told he would have to wait in the hall. Twenty minutes later he was called into the courtroom but his lawyer hadn't arrived yet. After several attempts to contact Mr. Pinkosky the judge decided to adjourn the trail until he could be located. Tyrone felt a sign of relief even if it was only until his lawyer could appear in court but it meant that he wouldn't be behind bars at least not today. Instead of taking the bus he took a cab back to Howard's.

CHAPTER FORTY-ONE

AFTER TELLING VANESSA about his condition he knew it was time he told his family. Calling his mother and telling her that he needed to talk to her about something important; caused panic in her voice.

"Howard is everything okay."

"It's best that we talk in person mom. I would like to invite everyone over for dinner next week."

"Well honey your sister and I will come but I'm not sure if I can get your father to come too."

"I don't want to get into the reason why I want you guys to come but just let him know that I really need to see him too and it would mean a lot to me if he could come."

"Okay I'll see what I can do baby."

"Mom, have you spoken to Uncle Steve lately?"

"Yes he is doing much better but he is still in rehab. Your dad and I visit him every week".

"Do you think they will allow him come with you next week when you come and see me?"

"I'm not sure because the program requires that he stays there for ninety days and it's not even been two months yet."

"Okay can you find out if he can leave and if he can't come then ask them if we all can meet there and talk?"

"Howard baby what is this all about you're starting to worry me?"

"Mom I'm not trying to make you worry but it would be best if I could talk to everyone at the same time."

"Okay I'll see what I can do and I'm not sure if I can talk your father into coming but I will try."

"Well just work your magic on him and I'm sure he won't say no."

"I'll talk to him and I will let you know by the end of the week."

"Okay thanks mom. I love you bye."

"Bye baby I love you too."

As Howard hung up the phone it pained him to think about how this was going to affect his mother once she found out that he was dying. Throughout the years after Howard had left home his mother had always tried to repair the relationship between her husband and her son but his father was so stuck in his ways that it was hard for him to forgive his son.

CHAPTER FORTY-TWO

AN HOUR AWAY in Milton, Dmitri was preparing for his trip to Toronto. Although his mother Theresa didn't want him to go; it was something he needed to do. Dmitri wanted to get to know his sisters and know more about who his father was. His mother wasn't able to have any more kids after she gave birth to him because of medical reasons.

The only memories that Dmitri had of his father was when he lived with them which ended just before his ninth birthday. His mother told him that his father was a dead beat dad and that he had left them to go back to his other family because he didn't love them anymore. The pain that his father caused his mother she took out on him because she blamed Dmitri for his father leaving. By the time his father was killed in the car accident Dmitri was twenty-one and his mother felt he had a right to know the truth. She had lots of pictures of them together, letters and birthday card that she kept from him and he was amazed at how much he looked like his dad. His mother explained everything to him from how they met right up until the day his father felt he had to go back to his wife and kids. However she never told him that his father wanted to be a part of his life because her heart wouldn't allow her to admit that he had left her and not him. His father was the only man she had ever truly loved and now the guilt of keeping Dmitri away from him for all those years was back to haunt her because he wanted to go and meet his sisters.

When Theresa found out that Quincy was dead she wanted to take Dmitri to the funeral but instead she went by herself and stayed in her car until everyone was gone before she went to say her final good-byes. She couldn't take the chance of anyone seeing her and asking who she was. Later she told him that she didn't know that his father had died until after he was buried, which was a lie since it was all over the news. His mother feared that the lies she told him would come to light once he meets his sisters. The love she had for his father had clouded her judgement because when he left her she didn't want him to have any part of Dmitri's life either. Never once did his father miss a child support payment and when he died his lawyer contacted Theresa and told her that Dmitri's college fees were paid in full.

When Dmitri arrived at Vanessa's it was after five and he decided to leave his overnight bag in the car just in case he didn't want to stay. He walked up to the house and rang the door bell. Not knowing who it was that answered the door he asked for Vanessa.

"Come on in you must be Dmitri?"

"Yes and are you Vanessa?"

"Oh no I'm Tracy, just a friend."

Tracy really needed to stop telling people that they were friends because although Vanessa had made her feel very comfortable they weren't friends but she wanted them to become friends. Dmitri followed her into the back yard and was surprised to see how many people were there; it seemed as if there was a party going on. As they walked out all eyes were on them and Vanessa and Rachel came over introduced themselves and gave him a big hug. After introducing him to everyone they excused themselves and went inside the house to talk. Howard was sleeping in the living room so Vanessa brought them into the kitchen. Vanessa insisted that Dmitri spend the night so that they could get to know each other better because it was hard for them to have a decent conversation with the loud music and she needed to get back to her guest.

Dmitri called his mother to let her know that he had arrived safely and he would be spending the night. After everyone had left the BBQ Vanessa, Rachel and Dmitri stayed up until two in the morning talking about their father. There was so much about him that Dmitri didn't know and it was nice to know that he wasn't as bad as his mother had made him out to be. However he was shocked to find out that his father had argued several times with his mother because she wouldn't allow him to visit his father's side of his family.

Vanessa arranged for Dmitri to sleep on the sofa bed as he lay trying to sleep he couldn't help thinking how wonderful Vanessa and Rachel had been. It was like they had known him all their lives. He also couldn't get Tracy off of his mind. She was absolutely stunning and he was glad he was able to get a chance to talk to her. It was just a shame she was pregnant. They didn't get a chance to talk very long but he did find out that the father of her baby was Howard. He was glad he didn't have to ask her about the situation because Vanessa had already told him that her husband cheated on her with Tracy. Within the short conversation that they did have he managed to find out that she was single and she gave him her number and that's all he needed to know. It was a strange situation to be in but there was something about this woman that made him want to get to know her more.

Dmitri wasn't an all around the world type of man he had only been with two women both long term relationships. One was for five years and the other was for two and a half years. Melanie was the love of his life but when she got an offer to work at one of the biggest publishing companies in the States she jumped at the offer.

For the first four months they sent e-mail, talked on the phone and he even went down to visit her during March break and twice after that but it was expensive to travel back and forth. Melanie became too busy to e-mail or talk on the phone because she was working during the days and working on her first book. After six months of trying to make the best of their relationship it was pretty much done when he met Sasha. Their relationship was hot and spicy because Sasha was a very shy person in public but a sexual freak in the bedroom. Anything he wanted her to do she did it; she introduced him to all her toys and told him her fantasy of having him bring a friend into the bedroom. He agreed only if the guy didn't touch him and if she would bring one of her friends and make it a foursome.

Two weeks later they were both able to find a friend that would agree; so they rented a hotel room with two queen size beds. The agreement was that only one man to a bed but the girls could both be on the same bed for fifteen minutes or less. This continued for several months until Dmitri found out that it was still going on behind his back. She was also sexually involved with her friend too; something she never did when he was around. When he ended the relationship she begged him not to leave but he felt that she had betrayed him and wondered how many more lies she was keeping from him.

With his eyes closed Dmitri turned onto his side, pulled the covers up to his shoulders and tried to sleep. Unable to sleep he decided to call Tracy although she was just in the spare room upstairs.

"I hope I didn't wake you?" Dmitri said.

Tracy wasn't sure who it was on the other end but he sure had a sexy voice. She checked the clock; it was after three but after the BBQ ended she just couldn't fall asleep.

"No I've been unable to sleep so I'm reading 'Act Like a Lady ~Think Like a Man'."

"Oh I heard the movie is better than the book have you seen it?"

"No. Still not sure who it was she said "By the way who is this?"

"Oh I'm sorry it's Dmitri."

Tracy was surprised because he didn't sound that way last night when they were talking but then again the music was so loud. After a long conversation Tracy told him she was going to try and get some sleep because she wanted to go to church in the morning. It was a place she hadn't been to in a long time but felt that it was time to start going again. When he asked if he could come with her she said yes. He then offered to take her to see 'Act Like a Lady ~Think Like a Man' and was glad when she said yes. Once he hung up the phone he jumped up and danced his way into the kitchen with a smile on his face.

"So what's that smile all about?" Vanessa asked as she sat drinking her morning coffee. Unable to hide his joy he decided to find out as much as he could about Tracy.

"First of all I must say that I have never felt so comfortable with anyone in my life. The both of you have made me feel as if we have known each other all of our lives. And secondly tell me more about Tracy."

Vanessa was shocked that he wanted to know about Tracy considering she was pregnant with Howard's baby. What could she actually tell him about her beside the fact that she was her husband's mistress.

"Oh so that's it. I seen you two talking last night and now you have that same smile on your face." Vanessa said.

Not able to remove the smile from his face he said "Well are you going tell me anything; like is she someone I should stay away from or is she a good person?"

"Honestly I really don't know her that well; so any information you want to know you're going to have to ask her yourself." She said then asked him if he wanted a cup of decaffeinated coffee."

"Actually I don't drink coffee but I'll have some tea with two sugars no milk." Vanessa put the kettle to boil. She sat down beside her brother and put her arm around his shoulder. She then told him how happy she was that he was there. Shortly after Tracy walked into the kitchen and Vanessa left them alone. She went into the living room to spend time with Howard and the girls.

CHAPTER FORTY-THREE

KNOWING THAT HE had to appear in court the next day and that the final nail would be put into his coffin Tyrone went to talk to Howard. As he sat next to Howard he could tell that he was glad to see him. Just by the way his pale face lit up when he entered the living room. They sat talking about how they met, work and their friendship. Howard then thanked him for not mentioning his name and how sorry he was that he couldn't be there for him. They also talked about Leroy and how they both felt guilty for his death. Tyrone told Howard about his sleepless nights and waking up in a pool of sweat, screaming, I'm sorry it was my fault. For the first time Howard could see the compassion in Tyrone's eye's as tears streamed down his face. It was hard for Tyrone to hold back the tears because he had already lost one friend and knew it was just a matter of time before Howard would be gone too.

The next morning Tyrone was back in court and glad that his lawyer was also there. They went over what was to be expected before entering the courtroom. There was no doubt in Tyrone's mind that he would be found guilty but at thirty-nine he prayed that he didn't get life. With Howard being the only one that could collaborate Tyrone's story it could go either way. After hours in the courtroom the judge called for a recess. Tyrone took the time to fine something to eat considering it could be his last proper meal in a long time. Instead of grabbing something from the café in the court house he went across the street to Swiss Chalet. After ordering his food he walked to the far back of the restaurant to sit down. However, that was a big mistake because Mrs. Anderson was there sitting with her daughter. As he turned to sit somewhere else he could see Mrs. Anderson standing up and he knew that he made the right decision. When Mrs. Anderson saw the son-of-a-bitch that was involved in the death of her son. Her heart was overwhelmed with pain;

knowing that she once not only cared for but loved Tyrone like a son. Now she hated him with a passion she never thought she could feel. Without saying a word Tyrone knew that he was not welcomed and took his food outside to eat on the patio. As he sat down to eat he bowed his head and said a silent prayer asking God to forgive him for everything that he had done. He was glad that he had expressed his feelings about everything that had happened with Howard; it was just a shame Howard wouldn't be around. He then realized the time; ate in a rush and went back because he didn't want to be late.

Once back in the courtroom it didn't take long for the jury to find him guilty of two accounts of murder with a life sentence. With tears in his eyes Tyrone looked back at Mrs. Anderson and mouthed the words "I'm so sorry" as he was handcuffed and taken away. He was then taken into the paddy wagon with the other prisoners and as much as he wanted to cry; he knew he couldn't. There was no way he would allow one tear to fall from his eyes as he sat down among six other men.

CHAPTER FORTY-FOUR

WITHIN THE NEXT couple of weeks Howard's condition worsened and more family members and friends were coming by to spend time with him. When Howard's mother, sisters and uncle stopped by for Sunday dinner; Vanessa was very disappointed when she opened the door and his father wasn't there.

Throughout the years Howard had tried to work on his relationship with his father especially after the twins were born. Since his father still refused to see or talk to him, he would send the girls to visit his parents on the weekend. However, when he found out the things his father was saying about him; he immediately stopped the girls from going. It was painful to have to tell him mother that they would no longer be spending the weekends but she understood, why after he told her what his father was doing.

They all gathered in the living room and had a lovely dinner under the circumstances. Mrs. Blackwood stayed by Howard's side the entire time she was there. It was excruciating to watch his mother talk about when he was younger because he could hear the crackling in her voice and knew she was on the verge of crying. Before leaving his mother was able to spend some alone time with him while everyone else went out for dessert. It was heart wrenching knowing the pain that he was causing his mother. When he told her everything about his condition, about Tracy and that he needed her to accept Tracy and his child as part of the family. He also told her that it would mean a lot to him if she could try again to convince his father to come and see him. Knowing her sons condition Mrs. Blackwood felt certain that it wouldn't be a problem to convince her husband to come and see their son.

The last four months after finding out about Howard's condition was very hard on Vanessa. By the time Howard finally agreed to have chemotherapy it was too late. Dr. Patterson wanted to put a metal tube or stent into his bile duct to prevent or relieve the blockage but by then the cancer had spread to other areas of his body. Watching her husband slip away was very painful and strenuous especially because she was pregnant. It was even harder seeing the girls having to deal with it as well.

With the amount of people that were visiting him; Vanessa had to take extra precaution to make sure that everyone wore a hospital gown, mask and used hand sanitizer. As weak as he was Howard enjoyed having people around him because it kept him happy. He knew that his time was coming to an end and with his love ones around him; he didn't have time to feel sorry for himself because being with them made him feel loved. Vanessa allowed the girls to stay home from school because she didn't want them to be away from their father. It was hard for everyone to watch as Howard slowly withered away. Vanessa was glad when she was able to convince the hospital to allow her instead of the other nurse to take care of him. What was even better she would also be getting paid for taking care of her husband considering their insurance was going to pay for a nurse to stay with him anyway. As overwhelming as it was Vanessa had many shoulders to lean on, even her brother who was now staying in the den where Tyrone had stayed. Being able to be there for Vanessa meant so much to him. They had lost too many years of each other's lives already and Dmitri felt honoured to be by her side when she needed so much support.

Dmitri and Tracy were spending a lot of time together and although she was pregnant with Howard child it didn't bother him because he loved kids. He even took her with him when he went home to get his computer and pick up some more clothes. It was a good thing that he owned his own online business because it allowed him to work from anywhere just as long as he had access to the internet. However his mother wasn't too happy when he showed up and introduced her to a pregnant woman especially because she could see that he had that look in his eyes. It was the same look she saw when he brought Sasha home. Pulling him into the kitchen as she told Tracy to take a seat in the living room. Theresa had to know who this woman was and why her son had that look in his eyes again. Theresa was shocked to hear the story behind her pregnancy and even more shocked that her son wanted to get involved with a woman like that. However after getting to know Tracy through the five hours that they were there she began to understand and even like her but just not for her son. Against his better judgement Dmitri allowed his mom to talk him into staying for dinner and by the time they were done Theresa insisted that they spend the night.

The next morning after breakfast Tracy and Dmitri were on their way back to Vanessa's before his mother could talk him into staying for lunch. The drive back to Toronto was very relaxing as they talked and learned a lot about each other's lives.

Tracy had a lot of issues but there was something about her that made Dmitri feel that she needed to be loved; it was in her eye and the way she told her life story. He enjoyed her company because she was so different from any other women that he had ever met before and the fact that she was pregnant and alone made him want to be with her even more.

When they arrived at Vanessa's she was in the living room with Howard. Dmitri went into the den while Tracy went upstairs to the spare room. After unpacking his bags Dmitri noticed that he had nine missed calls and they were all from his mother. As he dialed her number he walked into the kitchen and there was a note on the stove from Vanessa that said dinner was in the microwave."

"Hi mom is everything okay?"

"Yes I just wanted to make sure you got back safely. Why did it take you so long to call I was worried?"

"Mom please stop worrying about me so much; we made a few bathroom stops and I didn't realize that the ringer on my phone was off."

"I can't help it honey I miss you. So how long are you going to stay this time?"

"I miss you too Mom but you're acting as if I'm moving out, I'm just spending some time with my family and plus Vanessa really needs all the help she can get right now."

"I understand that but the house is so empty when you're not here."

"I know mom but it's not like I'm not coming back and I'm sure Kevin won't mind keeping you company while I'm gone."

Kevin was his mother boyfriend and although he wasn't the kind of man Dmitri wanted to see his mother with, he made her happy. They had only been dating for nine months but the changes he saw in his mother made him happy. Kevin was a construction worker and was also very handy with fixing all the problems around the house and whether she kept him around to get things fixed or she really liked him it didn't matter to Dmitri.

"That's not the point and you can't compare yourself with Kevin."

"I'm not but do you think I don't know that he came over last night. Why do you still feel that you have to hide the fact that he sleeps over from me? Mom I want you to be happy and if Kevin is that man than I'm happy for you."

"I wasn't hiding him he was still here when you left wasn't he?"

"Mom please don't treat me like a fool because you want me to believe that he arrived in the morning but I know better. So how is Kevin doing by the way?"

Theresa was grateful that her son wasn't standing in front of her when he asked that question because she honestly didn't think he heard Kevin coming in last night.

"He is fine he's been coming to keep me company since you've gone."

"Well that's a good thing you two can play house until I get back."

"Now Dmitri he sleeps on the couch". Although she was lying she didn't need her son knowing the truth.

"Mom you don't have to explain anything to me you are a grown women with needs and you don't have to pretend because I'm your son. Before she could reply Kevin came up behind her and wrapped his arms around her waist causing her to scream out.

"Mom what's wrong!"

"Oh nothing Kevin just scared me but I'm going to have to go now I'll talk to you soon. Bye honey I love you."

She hung up before Dmitri could say another word and turned her attention to the hardness that was pressing against the small of her back. Scooping her up in his arms Kevin picked her up and carried her up the stairs. Once upstairs he pushed the door open with his foot and gently dropped her on the bed. He then removed his jeans with a devilish look on his face as he continued to take the rest of his clothes off. As Theresa looked up into her lover's eyes she was overwhelmed by her love for him and she knew that it was time to let her protective wall down. She had been protecting her heart for so many years that she forgot how good it felt to be in love. Although she knew there was a possibility that she could be hurt again it was worth letting her guard down with Kevin and being in his arms made her forget everything else that was going on in her life. Surprisingly two days later Dmitri had to check his phone to make sure it was working because his mother had not called him and he couldn't help but wonder if everything was okay as he picked up the phone to call her.

"Hi mom is everything okay?"

"Yes why?"

"Well because I haven't heard from you in two days."

"I thought I would give you some space; so how are you doing?" she asked. There was laugher in the background and he knew that she wasn't alone he assumed it was Kevin.

"I'm good. Did I catch you at a bad time mom?"

"Actually you did but I'll call you later. I love you bye". As he hung up the phone there was a smile on his face because he knew his mother was being well taken care of in more ways than one.

CHAPTER FORTY-FIVE

VANESSA AND THE girls had been camping out in the living room so that they could be by Howard's side but that night the girls had slept in their beds while she stayed with Howard. she had also been taking lots of pictures and video footage daily of him and the girls. At five o'clock in the morning Vanessa got up to give Howard his medicine and realized that there was something terribly wrong with her husband. After checking his vital signs she knew she had to get him to the hospital as soon as possible. She started screaming as she dialled 9-1-1, within minutes the girls and Dmitri were by her side. Once the ambulance were gone Dmitri told the girls to get dress while he slipped on a pair of track pants before heading to the hospital.

On November 16 Howard Terrence Blackwood was rushed to the hospital; he was barely alive. Through all the excitement, Vanessa went into labour. Not wanting to be separated from her husband. She demanded that they be in the same room. The doctors positioned the beds so that Howard and Vanessa were head to toe. While holding onto his wife's hand Howard was able to watch his son enter a world he would soon be leaving. Vanessa looked over at her husband and saw that the reality of losing him was near. At that moment Vanessa knew that she was losing the love of her life. He was the only man that she had depended on in more ways than one for the past twelve years. He was her everything and the thought of him not being around to help her raise their kids was unimaginable. Their relationship was very rocky in the beginning because Vanessa wasn't sure if Howard was the right man for her; so she was still sleeping with other men. It wasn't until Howard found out that she was sleeping around that she realized how much he meant to her. Her life before Howard was filled with men that were either married or just wasn't ready to settle down. Not realizing how much damage she was doing to herself; she talked herself into believing that's what she needed because she didn't want anyone or anything to come between her and her career. It took Vanessa two months and three days to convince Howard that she only wanted to be with him. Eight months later they were married in a small church with only fifty family and friends to watch them say their I dos. He was the man that showed her how wonderful love could be and how easy it could be to melt into love. Vanessa gave birth to a seven and a half pound baby boy; they named their son Howard Quincy Blackwood. The concept of losing the love of her life was too overwhelming for her to handle, especially now that she had just given Howard the son he always wanted. Uncontrollably Vanessa started to cry, she cried silently like a little child because she didn't want Howard to hear or see her, but obviously it was impossible.

As he waited for Vanessa and Howard to be assigned to a room; Dmitri contacted Rachel. Who called Howard's mom, Lorraine, Kim and Omar. Howard's sisters, Steveroy and Richard where also there. In less than thirty minute they were all at the hospital to show their support. It was hard for everyone because it was truly a bitter sweet moment especially when the nurse came to tell them that Vanessa had a boy. Mrs. Blackwood was a nervous wreck after getting off the phone with her husband who refused to come to the hospital. Even on his sons dying bed her husband couldn't find it within himself to just be there for his son. For the past twenty-two years she missed out on so much of her sons life because of her husband. She was so lost in her thoughts that she didn't realize that everyone had walked off until her daughter said lets go mom. Not knowing where she was going she followed her daughter into Vanessa and Howard's room. The first thing Mrs. Blackwood did was look at her grandson, then kiss him on his forehead. As much as she wanted to hold him she need to be by her sons side so, she kissed Vanessa before going over to her son. She looked down at his frail body. All the life was drained from his body and she could hardly recognize her son. She didn't realize that she was crying until she could taste the salty tears enter her mouth.

They all gathered into the room with Howard and Vanessa after Howard Quincy Blackwood was born. He was named after Vanessa's dad which was also Dmitri's middle name. Omar decided that they should all bow their heads and pray because it was never too late for that. They all took hold of each other's hands. Vanessa was holding Howard's and Tonya, while he held hers and Tianna's hand. It continued on with Rachel, Omar, Lorraine, Steveroy and Kim. They each said a prayer for Howard; he even said a few words himself. Through it all, Vanessa was feeling a lot of discomfort because baby Quincy tore her so bad she had to get eight stitches but she tried to make everyone think she was just fine. Although she wanted something for the pain, Vanessa also wanted to be fully aware of what was going on just in case Howard needed her.

One hour before Howard and Vanessa's 10th anniversary, the doctor asked that everyone leave the room. Getting the twins to understand why they had to leave was hard for Rachel because it was obvious that their parents were in pain. After awhile the doctor drew the curtains between Howard and Vanessa because Howard's condition was getting worse. By now, Howard was so weak the doctors decided that it would be best if he got some rest.

Four hours later they were finally allowed to go back into the room, everyone surrounded the two beds as they talked and reminisced about old times, both good and bad. Vanessa asked the nurse if Quincy could also be in the room with them and after getting the okay from the doctor; she brought him in and placed him on the bed beside Howard. A few times the nurses had to come into the room to remind them to lower their voices. Because of Howard's condition they didn't want him to be overwhelmed with all the excitement that was going on.

As everyone talked amongst themselves, Howard could feel his life slowly slipping away. He then kissed his son on the forehead, looked around at everyone that loved him and closed his eyes. With his arm resting on his son; he thought about his father and how easy it was for him to turn his back on him. His heart ached as he thought about his mother, the girls, his son and Vanessa. He even thought about Tracy and the child she was having for him that he would never see. While taking his last breath he wanted to tell everyone 'Don't Waste the Years' but he wasn't able to. No one even noticed or got the chance to say good bye. It wasn't until the machine stopped that everyone's attention was drawn to him. At that precise moment, everyone began to panic. Not long after, the room was filled with doctors and nurses and they were asked to leave. They desperately tried to bring him back to life, but it was too late.

Vanessa stepped out of the bed to make her way over to her husband, but as she tried, two of the nurses took hold of her arms. Even though she was weak from giving birth nothing or no one was going to stop her from being by Howard's side. Not knowing how she did it, she managed to break free from the nurses. As she got onto the bed a nurse was about to pick up Quincy but in a firm voice she told her to leave him. They laid there as if Howard was sleeping peacefully. She held onto her dead husband's hand; while Quincy laid between them. Everything happened so quickly that the doctors had no choice but to leave her on the bed beside him. With tears in her eyes she tried to remain calm because she didn't want to make it any harder on herself. The doctor gave her a sedative so that she could relax. Not long after her eyes felt heavy and the only thing she remembered was the ceiling lights and hearing the nurses and doctors talking around her. However, she couldn't make out a word they were saying. Howard died after spending only an hour with his only son in his arms.

Quincy and Faith was born on the same day their father died and although Tracy wanted to be there with Howard; she wasn't able to because she went into labor while everyone was waiting to go back into the room. She was grateful that Dmitri came with her and between going back and forth from her room and Howard's he was mostly by her side. Three hours later she gave birth to a baby girl and Dmitri cut the umbilical cord. The doctor's were worried because her blood pressure was very high; especially after she heard that Howard was gone. For the remainder of the week Tracy stayed in the hospital because of her blood pressure. Vanessa on the other hand didn't want to leave the hospital she either slept or just laid there with her eyes wide open; unable to speak. The whole time she was wishing that it was all a bad dream, but after four days, she knew it was very real. She just laid there thinking about Howard, all the good times they had. Almost two week later she remembered that she had a son. She then pushed the button and a nurse came into her room, checked her blood pressure and brought Howard Quincy Blackwood to see his mother.

CHAPTER FORTY-SIX

RACHEL AND OMAR brought the girls back to her apartment after picking up some clothes, toys, their blankets and pillows; while Vanessa and the baby remained in the hospital. Rachel assumed that she would be able to comfort the girls in one way or another, but they wouldn't allow her to. They only wanted to know when they could see their parents. Rachel wanted to tell the girls that their father was gone but she thought it would be best if it came from their mother. She had gone to see her sister every night with Dmitri, Lorraine and Kim but there was, no changes she just laid there staring at the ceiling. With everything that had happened, to top it off their God father Tyrone was murdered in jail after only being there for three weeks. Rachel tried to keep it from the girls but it was all over the news.

The phone rang just when Rachel was finishing up the last of the breakfast dishes.

"Hello"

"Hi may I speak with Miss. Phillips, please?" Not knowing who it was she was hesitant to answer the lady on the other end.

"Yes this is she; how may I help you."

"It's Mrs. McCormack from the hospital. Your sister is asking to see you."

"Okay, thanks for calling I'll be there as soon as I can."

"I'll let her know. Bye".

Rachel hung up the phone with pure excitement rushing through her, she grabbed a dish cloth and dried her hands. Thankful that the girls were in the room she went into the living room to tell Omar.

"I just got a call from the hospital, Vanessa's awake and she wants to see me. So if you don't mind can you watch the girls?"

"Of course, are you going to be alright?"

"It's not me I'm worried about; I'm scared I won't be able to find the right words to say to her."

"Just listen to her. Don't lie about anything, but at the same time don't fill her up with too much information. She may not be able to handle it all at once."

"Yeah, I know. I'm just glad she is talking now, although it will be a long time before she will be alright again."

As he held her in his arms she didn't want him to let her go because she felt so safe. He then released her, kissed her softly on the forehead and without telling the girls that she was leaving she left. Twenty-five minutes later she arrived at the hospital a trip that should have only taken fifteen minutes but the traffic was extremely slow. After paying the parking meter she rushed into the hospital but instead of taken the elevator, she ran up the five flights of stairs to Vanessa's room only to find it empty. She walked out into the hallway, frantically looking for someone to help her; no one was in sight so she went down to the nurses' station.

"Excuse me! Would you be able to tell me where Vanessa Blackwood's room is please? She should be in room 515; do you know where I can find her?"

"Yes she is just down the hall to your left in the nursery."

"Thank you". Rachel walked in that direction, not knowing what to expect, when she entered the room Vanessa's back was facing her. Vanessa sat on the rocking chair with her son in her arms talking to him as if he could understand.

"I wish your daddy was here to see you; you look so much like him. He would be so proud of you; he always wanted a boy."

With tear filled eyes she continued to tell Quincy things about his father. Rachel walked up behind her and put her hand on her shoulder. Vanessa turned and was so happy to see her standing there. For the second time since everything happened, Vanessa was able to smile; she first smiled when she looked into her son's hazel eyes because they were identical to his fathers.

"Isn't he just beautiful? Howard would have loved him."

"I know he would have. When you first got pregnant, he would tell me how much he was praying for a boy."

Just then the doctor walked into the room.

"Excuse me; can I speak with you in the hallway for a moment please?"

He directed his question to Rachel, so she followed him into the hallway. As she walked off she looked at her sister with a questioning look on her face but Vanessa just shook her shoulder indicating that she didn't know what was going on.

"Hi I'm Dr. McNeil. Are you Mrs. Blackwood's sister?"

"Yes, I am."

"Well we have been trying to talk to your sister about what needs to be done with Mr. Blackwood's body, but she avoids the question and then changes the subject. Do you think you could have a talk with her? Something has to be done soon or we'll have to take matters into our own hands, and I know that's not what she wants."

"How much time does she have?"

"I can give her three days at the most, but if it can be done before that we would really appreciate it."

"Okay, Dr. McNeil, I'll have a talk with her. Is there anything else I can do?"

"We feel that she is ready to go home; your sister and the baby are doing fine. However, she feels that as long as her husband's body is still in the hospital she isn't leaving but we need her to make arrangements to have the body removed."

"Like I said I'll talk to her. Thank you for your concern."

"Everyone here is very worried about your sister. We've all worked with her over the years and wish her all the best. As well, we've set up a trust fund for the kids and her job will be here waiting for her whenever she is ready to return."

"Once again, thank you and I'll let her know."

They shook hands and he walked down the hallway while Rachel stood there thinking about what she was going to say to her sister. Since their parents died it was Vanessa, who kept her strong, when Roger was abusing her it was Vanessa that gave her the strength to leave and realize that she deserved better. It was now her turn to return the favour and be strong for her, although she didn't know how she was going to do it but she knew she had to find a way.

CHAPTER FORTY-SEVEN

AS MUCH AS Kim loved Richard and thought that she wanted to be with him; sexually she needed more. So when Mike a regular caller on her sex line wanted to meet up with her, she eagerly agreed. Mike flew in from New York and after having a lovely dinner they went to his hotel to have drink at the bar. Two hours and quite a few drinks later Kim was feeling very horny but she wasn't drunk enough not to know what she was about to do. He invited her back to his room and they continued to drink and before long Kim was on her knees polishing his manhood. Several positions later Kim was exhausted but knew she had to get up and go home before Richard wondered where she was. Mike on the other hand wanted more so she promised him that she would come back tomorrow afternoon and spend the day with him. When Richard arrived home and didn't see Kim he called her to find out where she was.

"Hi babes where are you, I just got in?"

"I'm on my way home now I'll be there soon."

"Okay can you stop at the drug store and pick up some condoms we used the last one this morning?"

"Didn't you just buy some the other day?" she said.

"Yes and your horny little ass used them all?"

"Wait a minute so I'm the horny one and all this time I thought it was you?" Richard broke out in a fit of laughter and then told her to get her ass home so he could punisher her for letting him use all the condoms on her sweet pussy. Before she could reply he hung up. This was the first time Kim cheated on Richard and the way Mike worked her pussy all she wanted to do was go home and take a hot bath because she was so sore. However there was no way she could tell Richard she didn't want to have sex because that was something she never did. He would defiantly know something was up. Twenty minutes later when Kim walked in Richard was in the shower so she went into the half bathroom and brushed her teeth, washed her face and cleaned herself just in case Richard got to her before she was able to take a shower. Being with Mike was great and she couldn't wait to see him again tomorrow. However, knowing that Richard would be pleasuring her with his tongue turned her on because that was something Mike didn't do. As sore as she was she gave Richard everything he wanted then fell asleep in his arms. Kim continued to see Mike every day for almost two months. She was starting to have feeling for him but she didn't want to lose Richard. Kim wanted to have her cake and eat it too. Mike on the other hand needed to go back home but wanted to continue to see Kim occasionally. However, when she told him it was over because she didn't want Richard to find out; he lost it. That night when she was in the bathroom he went into her purse and got her address.

Couple days later he finally found the courage to drop by her place and he didn't care if her boyfriend was there or not. He knocked hard on the door and Kim's first thought was that it was the police. Without looking through the peephole she opened the door. When she saw Mike she was not only shocked but scared. By the look in his eyes she knew it would a bad idea not to check who it was before opening the door. He then pushed his way in and convinced her that he only wanted to talk but that was far from the truth. He pounced on her like a tiger and as much as she wanted to resist; she was turned on by his forcefulness. They did the nasty on the king size bed Richard bought for them. When they were done he asked her if she was sure she wanted to stop seeing him and when she said yes. He got dressed without saying a word and left.

The next day Mike waited outside Kim's apartment building but this time he waited for Richard to come out, he had seen a picture of him when he was in the apartment. So he knew exactly who he was looking for. When he saw Richard he got out of his car and confronted him. He told him that he had been sleeping with Kim for the past two months. That he had fucked her on their king size bed and cleaned up with his blue and white towel that hung on his side of the sink. Mike then handed him a printed copy of the picture he took of Kim pleasuring him on her knees. Richard was outraged by what he was hearing and when he saw the picture he felt sick to his stomach. Unable to speak Richard left Mike standing there with a smile on his face.

When Kim arrived home that night she was surprised to see that Richard was home so early. As soon as she looked at him she knew something was wrong so she went over to him.

"Hi babes, is everything okay?"
"No!"
"Why what's wrong?"
"Do you love me?"
"Of course, you know I do."

"Remember when I told you I loved you and you told me that I was the first man that has ever said that to you?"

"Yes."

"Don't I make you happy?"

"Babes you know you do, I've never been happier."

"Then why would you cheat on me! I have left my wife and son to show you that it's you I want to be with and you do this to me?" Kim was speechless as Richard threw the picture in her face and walked out of the apartment.

When Richard walked out on her; he took a piece of her heart with him and the only way she could stop thinking about him was to be with Mike. After asking Rachel if it was okay if she brought Mike to her wedding; she then asked Mike if he wanted to come with her. When she asked him to come to the wedding with her; he insulted her by saying "What would I want with a woman that would cheat on me" he then slammed the phone in her ear.

Kim's fear of commitment and her need for sex left her with exactly what she never wanted which was to be alone.

CHAPTER FORTY-EIGHT

WHEN DR. PATTERSON heard about Howard's death, he did exactly what Howard wanted him to do, which was to deliver a package with three separate envelops to his lawyer. One had the lawyer's name on it; the other two had Vanessa and Tracy's, indicating that the lawyer's envelope should be opened first. Although Dr. Patterson never opened the package, he could tell that there were two video cassettes inside along with some papers. He assumed that the envelopes contained the way Howard wanted his Will to be handled once he was gone. Once he arrived at the lawyer's office, the secretary told him that he was with a client, but would be right with him shortly; so she offered him a coffee while he waited. After making his coffee, he grabbed a muffin and sat down to wait.

Twenty minutes later, a well dressed tall black man with a slight sign of greying hair walked over to him and introduced himself as Raymond Boston. He then indicated for him to come into his office. Once inside his office Raymond asked

"How may I help you?"

"I'm Dr. Patterson. I was Howard Blackwood's doctor before he passed."

By the look on the lawyer's face, Dr. Patterson could see that he didn't know and before he could continue Raymond cut him off.

"What! When did he die? His wife hasn't said a word to me and we've been friends for years" said Raymond.

"Well unfortunately, she's in the hospital as well. She delivered the same day he died."

"When and how did he die?"

"He passed away last week from cancer."

"Has he been buried yet?"

"I'm not sure; they won't let anyone in to see her besides family. I only heard about it because my assistant is a friend of his wife."

"Was there something I could help you with"?

"About four month ago, Howard came into my office. He left a package with me for you and two other for his wife and someone else name Tracy with strict instruction to give it to you once he passed."

He handed him the package, said good bye and left. Raymond Boston sat in his leather chair behind his desk; he placed the two envelopes and the package on his desk. He sat staring at his desk remembering his friendship with Howard, there was so much about him that made him such a great friend to have and he would miss him dearly. He picked up the envelope with his name on it and opened it.

Dear Raymond,

Well, if you're reading this letter; it means we won't be having any more drinks together. So let's get straight to the point. What I want you to do is give my wife and Tracy the package with their names on it in two weeks following my death. Inside the package there is a video cassette as well as four hundred and fifty thousand dollars cash. I need you to change it into a cashier's check. Give Vanessa three hundred thousand and Tracy on hundred and fifty. I know that at this point you don't know who Tracy is but I really don't want to get into that, plus I'm sure you will hear all about it anyways. Let them know it's from some insurance policy that I took out with you; I trust that you will do as I asked and make sure that my family receives the money once I am gone. I also need you to be there for her, just make sure that she and the kids are fine. Dr. Patterson will be sending you a check once my wife and Tracy have received their package; I would like you to take your son on vacation because I know it's something you have been wanting to do. Thank you and have a great life; make the best of it; you never know when your time will be up. So live every day to its fullest and Don't Waste the Years.

P.S. Don't take this the wrong way; but if for Any reason they doesn't receive the money Dr. Peterson will be giving you a call.

Love always Howard

Raymond walked over to his wall safe and put the package inside. Once he was back at his desk, he picked up the phone and called his secretary.

"Hi Linda can you cancel all my appointments for the rest of the day and once your done you can take the day off."

As he spoke she could tell that he had been crying.

"Is everything alright Mr. Boston?"

"It's nothing for you to worry yourself about, just go home and enjoy those beautiful kids of yours because that's what I'm going to do. I will see you in the morning bye" said Raymond.

"Bye Mr. Boston" replied Linda.

For the next hour Raymond sat in his chair, crying for the loss of his dear friend and just reminiscing about all the good times they had spent together. He then went over to his ex-wife and spent the night with his son.

CHAPTER FORTY-NINE

RACHEL SAT WITH her sister trying to explain to her why it was time for her to make a decision as to what she wanted to do with Howard's body. After having to raise her voice and grabbing Vanessa by the shoulders and shaking her. She was finally able to get an answer out of her.

"Okay, Rachel. We'll arrange for the funeral to be next Saturday and I will let the doctor know I'm ready to go home."

"Now that that's settled, let me hold that handsome little boy of yours." Reluctantly, Vanessa handed the baby to her sister, then stood and walked over to the window.

"I don't know if I can handle all of this. I don't want everyone to feel sorry for me and tell me what a great person he was because I already know."

"I know it's going to be hard, but I'll be there for you as well as everyone else that loves you and the kids."

"How are the girls doing?"

"They're just fine. Omar's taking them to the movies then for dinner. I tried to explain to them, but I really think it needs to come from you; for them to really understand what's going on."

"I don't know what I'm going to say to them. If it was up to me I would never leave this room because I know once I do everything becomes real again. I'm not ready to face anyone right now and I don't want anyone's pity."

"All you need to know is that I will be here for you as long as you need me. How about we go for a walk and visit Tracy. Did you know she had a baby girl the same day Quincy was born."

"No! How is she doing?" Vanessa replied.

"I'm not sure. Did you want to go and see her?"

Following a long pause Vanessa finally agreed to go. Between the three of them they managed to arrange Howard's funeral by composing a list of people that needed to be called. They also decide to have an open casket, how many flowers they needed as well as everything else that had to be done. For the first time since everything happened, Vanessa felt a great sigh of relief lifted off of her shoulders. She felt that now she could leave the hospital and face the kids as well as the rest of the world. By the next day, Vanessa was willing and able to leave the hospital with Howard Jr. in her arms. After getting a call from Rachel, Lorraine took a quick shower and then headed over to Vanessa's with Steveroy to clean up the house before she came home from the hospital. When they pulled up to the house Kim, Richard and Dmitri were waiting for them on the front porch.

Between the five of them they managed to clean the house from top to bottom within four hours. Making sure they got rid of all of Howard's medical machines, medicine and put the living room back in order. While the girls cooked dinner, Dmitri, Steveroy and Richard fixed a few things that were broken around the house. By the time Vanessa, the baby and Rachel arrived after six everything was back in order and Omar was on his way over with the twins. It was a rough night with everyone walking around on egg shells not knowing what to say to Vanessa but overall by the time everyone left Vanessa felt scared but comfortable to tell the girls about their father.

It was hard for Vanessa to make the girls understand that they were never going to see their father again because they just couldn't understand why he would leave them in the first place. She then told them that he was in heaven and that he would always be with them even if they couldn't see him. They still didn't completely understand but they were too tired to ask any more questions and went to sleep. They all slept in the king size bed; where she once slept with her husband.

CHAPTER FIFTY

TRACY ON THE other hand felt lost within herself, although Dmitri had been there in the delivery room; she still felt that she had no one but her beautiful daughter which she name Faith. It was such a shame that Howard wasn't able to hold his daughter before he had passed. It didn't matter to her that Howard was married he belonged to her long before Vanessa. He had been the only man she ever truly loved and now he was gone. In the past months since finding out that he was dying, they had gotten very close again while she was staying in his house. With everything that was going on Tracy wasn't completely prepared to take Faith home because she hadn't had the time to pick up the rest of things she needed.

She knew it was hard for Vanessa to allow her husband's mistress to come into their home. However she had open up her home and her heart to allow Tracy to spend time with Howard and for that reason alone she was very grateful. Vanessa was a very special person because not many other women would look beyond the hurt and pain their husband had caused them and opened up their home and heart to her. She also knew that as hard as it was going to be; Vanessa wanted the kids to grow up knowing what a wonderful person their father was. Overall she was amazed at how Vanessa had included her in Howard's funeral arrangements. By the end of the next three days all the funeral arrangements were done, the girls and Vanessa were booked to see a counselor and Tracy and Faith were moving in. There was no doubt in Vanessa's mind that she wanted to try and make the living arrangement work with Tracy and her, because the girls loved having her and Faith around and it's what Howard wanted.

The day of the funeral was almost a month after Howard passed and it was the hardest day of Vanessa's life. There was an overwhelming amount of people that packed the church and streets of Yonge Street. Mrs. Blackwood was amazed that there were so many people that gathered for her sons funeral and at that precise moment she realized that she no longer cared if her husband was there or not; just as long as she was. She also knew that she wasn't ever going to try and forgive him for not going inside the church. There were several police cars escorting the guest to the church and then to the cemetery. Vanessa was glad that she decided to have an open casket and hearing the kind words that were being said about Howard made it twice as hard considering a lot of people were also asking about Tracy. Having to face all of those people that knew and loved her husband weakened her heart. Vanessa felt like she was having an out of body experience; as if she was hovering above everyone looking down hoping that at some point she would wake up and Howard would still be alive. As friends and family came by to comfort her with their words she learned a lot about the man she loved that she never knew.

Back at the house Vanessa welcomed as much people that could fit inside and in the back yard. It pained Vanessa's heart when she saw Howard's mother, sisters and his uncle but not his father walk into the house. Throughout their marriage Howard had spoken many times about his family and had also tried to mend things with his father. He always invited his family to every birthday party they had for the girls, Christmas and thanksgiving dinners but only his mother and sisters would come. Even when Howard would send his father a birthday present he would send it back; after awhile he just gave up. However Vanessa was shocked to see Mr. Blackwood at the funeral because even after he found out about his sons condition he never came by to see him. Before he passed Howard asked her to write a letter to his mother and father with strict instructions to give it to them once he was gone. When she saw Mrs. Blackwood she got the letters out of the computer desk, asked her where her husband was and handed her the letter with mom on it. When Mrs. Blackwood told her that he was still outside it made Vanessa's blood boil. With the letter in her hand she went outside to look for him; only to found him sitting in his car. When he saw her approaching; he came out of his car. Vanessa walked up to him and handed him the letter; she couldn't even look into the eyes of the man that had caused her husband so much pain and when he tried to speak to her she walked away. He was deeply hurt by her actions and too ashamed to go inside because he had allowed his pride to get in the way of loving his son. Instead of going into the house Mr. Blackwood called his wife on her cell phone to tell her that he was leaving and that she should take a cab home.

By the end of the day Vanessa was mentally and physically drained and was very grateful that her sister was taking all three kids back to her place for the weekend and that Tracy had gone back to her apartment. Having the house to herself was painful but also a relief because she was able to just take it all in without anyone around her; it was the first time since she left the hospital that she was alone and it actually felt good. Vanessa decided to take a hot bath before heading to bed; once she was done she took two sleeping pills and before she knew it she was out like a light.

CHAPTER FIFTY-ONE

WHEN HOWARD'S FATHER heard about his sons condition he had collapsed on the floor crying as he repeated 'Don't Waste The Years'. It was something his father always used to say to him and still he managed to lose all those years with his son. Even after he knew about his condition he still refused to talk to his son. Although, he wanted to his pride held him back from going to see him and two days later he found out that his son was gone. After bury his son Mr. Blackwood was just a mere shell lost within himself. When Vanessa handed him the letter with Dad on the front without looking at him then said "Your son wanted you to have this." It was like a slap in the face as she walked off when he was about to say something.

Mrs. Blackwood stood staring intensely at the letter in her hand and was startled by her cell phone ringing in her purse. After speaking with her husband she felt sick to her stomach as she hung up the phone on him when he told her she should take a cab home because he was leaving. As much as she wanted to read the letter now, it wasn't the right time or place. Several hours letter she was taking the letter out of her purse as she sat in the cab.

Dear mom,
If you're reading this it means I'm no longer with you. Mom you have been my rock throughout the years and I have always looked up to you. You have always stood by your kids even after I left you were always there for me. I never blamed you for any of this but I did respect you even more for standing up to him; even if it meant I still had to leave. Because of him you

have missed out on so many years of my kids life and I ask that you be there for them now; they will need you more than ever. Tell them about me and teach them all that you have taught me because they are always asking about you. Words can't even begin to say how much I love you and don't be angry because I'm gone; just hold onto the years that we had.

I will forever Love mom
bye

When Mr. Blackwood arrived home he went into his room locked the door and sat on his bed to read the letter.

Dear Dad,

If you're reading this it means I'm no longer with you. I never really understood how things got so bad between us when you were the only person I looked up to. You taught me so much but in the end you took it all back when you wouldn't allow me to become my own person. I remember the stories that you used to tell us about your father. How he used to always tell you "Don't waste the years". When I asked you what he meant by that you told me that your father was a different kind of man and as much as he loved his kids he lived for himself. You then told me that when you turned fifteen your father packed his things to leave but before he left. He told you that while he was trying to be someone he wasn't and living day by day he realized that he had lost the years of his life by being what everyone else wanted him to be. That's the day you found out that your father was gay and when you gave me the keychain that he gave you that read 'My Imperfections Are What Makes Me Who I Am . . . Simplyme'. I thought that was your way of telling me you wanted me to be the person I wanted to be. But now I see that I was wrong because when I didn't want to be who you wanted me to be you turned your back on me.

I never stopped loving you dad and I only wished that you hadn't 'Wasted The Years by being mad *at me for something that was my choice to make. I have lived my life by loving those around me and respecting them for who they are; I only wish that you could have done the same. You missed out on a lot and I can only pray that your pride doesn't stop you from being there for me in the end.*

Love always your son
Bye dad.

    As Mrs. Blackwood read her letter there was a puddle of tears in her lap and she was lost within herself until the cab driver pulled her out of her thoughts to let her know she was home. Like a zombie she walked into the house and called out to her husband. When he didn't answer she went upstairs only to find the door lock. After reading his letter Mr. Blackwood locked himself inside his room; even when his wife was banging on the door he wouldn't let her in. As the days passed he refused to leave the house. He ordered cases of alcohol to be delivered and he would only leave the room to get food or meet the delivery boy at the door for his alcohol. The only fresh air he got was when he stuck his head out the window. With a bathroom in his room he didn't even want his wife to sleep in the bed with him. Like the years; Howard Sir's life was wasted as he withered away drinking and barely eating. Mrs. Blackwood was disgusted by her husband's behavior but at the same time looking at him just reminded her of the pain he had caused her son. Throughout the years she had had many disagreement with him about how he was treating their son and she always begged him to put his pride aside but he never did. Losing her only son and knowing that he died without his father by his side made her realize that her love for her husband died that day too. Mr. Blackwood couldn't face his wife knowing that even when she pleaded with him to come to the hospital that day he refuse to go. He spent the last weeks of his life locked in his room and passed away one month after his son from alcohol poison and was buried next to him.

    Mrs. Blackwood had lost her husband years ago when he allowed her son to walk out of his life. After Howard left he wasn't the same man that she married and yet he couldn't find it within himself to talk to his son again. Their marriage fell apart but she stayed with him regardless because she loved him even though she had lost all respect for him. As much as she felt pain for the loss of her husband; she also felt free from a marriage that held her back and unlike her son she didn't have the courage to leave. Now that her son was gone she needed to be a part of her grandkids lives. So that she could enjoy the rest of her life with them because unlike her husband she wasn't about to waste the years she had left.

CHAPTER FIFTY-TWO

VANESSA AND TRACY walked into Raymond's office unaware of what he wanted to talk to them about and waited in the waiting room. Ten minutes later he came out and asked Vanessa to come in; as she walked in he hugged her and told her to have a seat.

"How have you been Vanessa?"

"It's been hard especially with the baby and the girls but they keep my mind very busy."

"Well you know my ex-wife owns her own daycare centre and I can arrange for all three kids to be registered if that's alright with you. As well if there is anything I can do to help just let me know."

Vanessa was reluctant to answer so Raymond continued.

"Well that's something you can think about but let's get to the reason I asked you here. Howard came into my office one day and asked me to write up a Living Will, he never told me why but after he passed Dr. Patterson came to visit me. He left me three packages for me, you and Tracy. Now when I opened my package it gave strict instructions about how he wanted me to handle his insurance policy. I wanted to talk to you first but if it's okay with you I would like to call Tracy to come in?"

"I know that you may not know and understand everything that's going on with Tracy but we have become friends. Although the reason why we became friends was very stressful it's what Howard would have wanted."

"Is that a yes?"

"Yes it is."

Raymond picked up the phone and told his receptionist to tell Tracy to come in. After she took a seat Raymond gave them both their package and sat back. Simultaneously they opened their package and read the letter Howard wrote them.

To my loving wife,

My darling Vanessa if you're reading this it means I'm no longer with you and the kids. You have been my rock through thick and thin and I'm so proud to have been your husband. I'm sorry for the pain that I caused you but please I know that I never stopped loving you. My love for you goes beyond words and I can only pray that you can forgive me for my mistakes.

Please let the kids know how much they truly meant to me and I only hoped that I got a chance to meet my unborn child before my time was up. Take good care of our kids and always let them know how much I loved them. Continue to give them a kiss good night but when you do give them one for me too. I know that I'm asking a lot of you but I need my kids to grow up together as a family. I've seen how well you and Tracy get along and I hope it wasn't just a show. However, I do understand why you may not want to be good friends with her but don't stop the kids from being a part of their lives. I have left you with three hundred thousand dollars and I can only suggest that you take one hundred and pay off the house, my insurance from work will take care of the girls college fees, so set up another one for our child and please buy yourself that diamond ring we saw in Tiffany's.

PS I hope we had a boy
Love always Howard
Bye.

Dear Tracy,

If you're reading this it means I'm no longer with you and our child. When I think about how we met and all the fun times we used to have it brings back good memories. You helped me in so many ways to become the person I became. The love we shared was like no other I've ever had it was carefree and that's what kept us going. I've always had a weakness for you and that is what brought us to where we are now.

I know that I'm asking a lot of you but I need my kids to grow up together as a family. I've seen how well you and my wife got along and I hope it wasn't just a show. I'm not asking you to be best friends just please don't stop the kids from being a part of each other's lives.

I'm sorry for the way I treated you and I should have never used you the way I did. Please forgive me and take good care of our child.

PS. It was a blessing in disguise the day I bumped into you.
Lover always Howard
Bye

Both Vanessa and Tracy cried uncontrollably as they sat there looking at the letter. As much as Vanessa wanted to know what was in the letter Howard wrote to Tracy she knew she had no right to ask to see it. After signing some papers Vanessa and Tracy left Raymond's office, puffy eyed and holding hands.

EPILOGUE

FOUR MONTHS AFTER Omar asked Rachel to marry him, she still kept it a secret from her sister. With everything that had happened with Howard she just couldn't find the right time to tell Vanessa that she was not only engaged but also pregnant. She was grateful that she wasn't showing when she met Vanessa; after a lovely lunch she told her everything. It was an overwhelming feeling when she saw the excitement and joy in her sister eyes; a look she had not seen in a long time. Omar on the other hand had told his family, friends and co-workers right away because he couldn't contain his excitement of being a father. He loved his nieces and nephew but Rachel had always been the women he wanted to have kids with.

Since Rachel didn't want to give up her apartment and just move in with Omar they agreed that they would start looking for a new house, have a small wedding and then once the baby was born they would have a destination wedding in Jamaica.

Life without Howard left Vanessa with many sleepless nights and many times it was hard to get out of bed. Once she realized the pain it was causing the kids she knew it was time to get herself together and work toward their future without Howard. It took her much longer than she thought it would to return back to work but once she did it was as if she never left. She was grateful that the hospital allowed her to come back on modified hours so that she could pick up the kids on time from daycare. Now that the girls were in school all day Raymond not only arranged for the kids as well as Faith to be registered in his ex-wives daycare free of charge, he also arranged for the girls to go to the school in the area.

When Rachel told her that Omar had asked her to marry him and that she was pregnant it was the best news she had heard in a very long time. She was so happy for her sister and Omar because their love went back decades and with so many obstacles they still found a way to be together.

Although Dmitri's relationship with Tracy was going very well and he loved her daughter like his own; he wanted their relationship to move to another level. Spending time with her and Faith was great but he needed sex, badly and cheating on her wasn't an option. So instead of going back home he decided to stay and find his own apartment because living with Vanessa wasn't what he wanted to do. After deciding to take over Lorraine's lease on her apartment once she left; Dmitri went home to pack his things and tell his mother that he would be staying in Toronto. Dmitri thought that if he told his mother he was looking for an apartment closer to his sisters it would be hard on her but surprisingly she didn't put up much of a fight because Kevin was moving in with her. He spent two weeks with his mother getting his things together and helping Kevin move in. When Rachel asked Dmitri to give her away at her wedding he was honoured, they had come such a long way and both his sisters had opened up their hearts to him; he only wish that they hadn't wasted all those years. When he invited his mother and Kevin to come to Jamaica with him she was ecstatic, the only place his mother ever went, was to Cuba with his father.

Knowing that his partner would be able to manage the Toronto office Steveroy was looking forward to opening up another FAM Life Clothing Line in California. It was hard to believe that his clothing line which stood for 'Fearless Attitude Motivates Life' was doing so well. With two other locations one in Jamaica and the other in New York it was time to expand. Lorraine had given him some brilliant ideas that he wanted to implement into the California line and since their relationship was moving in the right directions he knew that he needed her by his side. She had not only made an impact on his life but also on his daughter, Jada.

When Steveroy invited Lorraine to go with him and his daughter to California, she was ecstatic and jumped at the opportunity. Lorraine loved the idea of being with him but she had a lot of loose ends to tie up before she could leave. She suggested that Jada stay with her, while he finds somewhere for them to live and registers Jada into school; he agreed that it would be the best thing to do and two weeks later they were saying their good-byes as Steveroy boarded the airplane. His plan was to only stay for three months, however, it took him almost six months before he could find a suitable location; where they could live and register Jada into school. By the time he did get back there wasn't much time left to pack and arrange for everything to be shipped to California before their trip to Jamaica for Rachel and Omar's wedding.

After Howard passed it was hard for Tracy to look at her daughter and not think about him. All the good and bad times they spent together but being in the house with Vanessa and the kids really helped her in so many ways because she and Vanessa became each other's rock. She stayed with Vanessa for five months before she decided it was time to take her baby girl home. Although Vanessa and Tracy were forced together because of Howard it didn't interfere with them becoming good friends. It wasn't just because of the kids or because Howard wanted them to get along they actually liked and respected each other. When Vanessa told her that Howard's friend Raymond arranged for Faith to have full time daycare it was a big relief because her maternity leave was over in three weeks. She had decided to take her maternity leave when she was six month, so that she could spend time with Howard and now that Faith was almost six months it was time to go back to work.

Her relationship with Dmitri was better than any other relationship she ever had considering they weren't having sex. With her being pregnant and then having to take care of Faith; they were able to get to know each other on a different level other than sexually. Dmitri knew what she wanted and need from a man, her secrets, her fears, her past and her goals. Although there was a lot of kissing, cuddling and foreplay he never pushed her to go any further and she respected him for that. Now that they were going to Jamaica for Rachel's wedding she thought it would be the perfect time for them to have sex; considering they would be sharing a room.

Date: May 27 2012
Time: 3:00pm
Location: Ocho Rios, Jamaica

    On the sunny island of Jamaica Rachel and Omar said their 'I dos' with Vanessa as her maid of honor and Kim, Lorraine and Tracy as her bride's maids while Dmitri gave her away. Omar had Gary his high school friend as his best man, Steveroy and two of his cousins as his groom's men. Omar wanted Richard to be one of his groom's men but he was shocked when he said no. However he was even more shocked when Rachel told him that Richard and Kim were no longer together because she cheated on him and that the guy showed Richard picture of them together in the bed he bought for them. He was glad that Richard left Kim but what really made Omar mad was when Rachel told him she had the nerve to want to invite the guy to their wedding. After finding that out Omar didn't want Kim at their wedding but she was Rachel's friend. Although he still kept in contact with Richard, seeing Kim made him sick to his stomach.

Vanessa's memories of her husband were brought back to life as she remembered the time they spent in Jamaica almost three years ago. If only she had known that it would have been their one and only vacation together. There were days since he was gone that the memories filled her heart and every time she thought of a bad memory she would push them away. At first it was hard to look at Tracy without thinking about what he had done and then there was Faith who looked so much like the twins. However; the lesson within all the pain was that it had taken too much out of her to be angry all the time. She also learnt that it was just easier to forgive and move on with her life instead harboring all that pain. Howard would always be the love of her life and she wasn't going to allow any bad memories to interfere with the man he was because there was always two sides to every story. When she thought about how their life was; she knew that she couldn't blame it all on Howard. Although he had made the decision to cheat on her, there was a reason why he cheated and she had to take some of that blame in order to move on with her life. Living without him was hard but she had so many people around her that loved and cared a lot about her and the kids. Little Howard was a spitting image of his father and Mrs. Blackwood had become a big part of their lives by taking them every other week. Vanessa even paid for Mrs. Blackwood and Mrs. Bedford's flight so that they could help out with the kids during the wedding. Their hands were full with Vanessa's three kids, Rachel's son Omar Tristan Jones Jr., Tracy's daughter Faith and Steveroy's daughter Jada. With all the activity at the resort they were able to manage while the grownups did grownup things. It was nice seeing her sister so happy; Omar and Rachel were meant to be together it was in her eyes years ago and it was still there now. Vanessa knew that Omar would also do anything and everything to make Rachel happy and it was in his eyes too. Before leaving Jamaica Vanessa and Mrs. Blackwood took the kids, Tracy and her daughter to meet Howard's family. She also spent some alone time with just the girls while Mrs. Blackwood watched her only grandson.

Her sister's wedding was the most beautiful wedding she had ever been to; she only wished Howard and her parents could have been there to enjoy the day with them. Vanessa, the kids, Mrs. Blackwood and Mrs. Bedford stayed for a month before going back to reality.

Lorraine's life with Steveroy and Jada had come a long way and she was now happy; although she wasn't able to have any kids of her own she was glad she had Jada. Jada's mother had given full custody to Steveroy so that she could move on with her life. This made Lorraine excited about their plans to move to California; even though it meant leaving everyone and everything behind it was a chance she was willing to take. She was shocked when Jada asked her dad when he was going to marry her but even more shocked that his reply was "very soon honey." This time in Jamaica was even better than the first because they were there as a family and they would be going to visit his family before they left. However she was looking forward to going to California and starting a new life with Steveroy and Jada.

He had showed her pictures of their new studio apartment on the internet and it was beautiful. He was leaving her in charge of doing all of the decorating; it had four bedrooms, a huge office on the main floor and the kitchen was to die for, with the biggest island she had ever seen. After Rachel's wedding they spent a week with his family before leaving for California.

The jealousy Kim felt toward Rachel and Omar was her own fault; she had ruined the only true relationship she ever had. Two days after the wedding she decided to go home. She just couldn't stand the way everyone was looking at her especially Omar. She now realized that her uncle had paved a path of destruction for her because it was hard for her to believe that any man could love. He made it hard for her to believe that she could be happy with a man even if they loved her. She also thought that having sex made her happy and the more she had the happier she would be but now she realized how much that wasn't true. It was Richard that made her happy, that showed her that she was worthy of being loved and how much it meant to him to show her he loved her.

She had tried to talk to him, make him understand how sorry she was but he was done with her. She could hear the pain in his voice and that was the worst pain of all knowing how much she had hurt him. Once she was back home she decided that it would be best to go spend some time with her mother and take some time off of work; maybe even tell her mother about uncle Ronny.

Being with Dmitri and getting to know him in a way that she has never known any other man before; allowed Tracy to fall in love for the second time in her life. The night after the wedding Dmitri and Tracy made love for the first time and it was better than he ever imagined. They stayed for two week then went back because Tracy had to work. His mother and Kevin left the same day as well. Dmitri was looking forward to living with Tracy and Faith. He was also glad that he could move on with his life knowing that his mother was happy with Kevin.

For the first time in her life Rachel was the one taking care of Vanessa. Watching her sister deal with losing Howard was very hard. When their parents died Vanessa took care of her; now she had to be Vanessa's rock. As happy as she was with Omar she felt guilty for being happy when her sister was falling apart. She was however glad that Vanessa had a lot of people around her to help with the kids and help keep her from constantly thinking about Howard.

Before leaving for their wedding Rachel and Omar purchased their first house, just a fifteen minute drive away from her sister. The day of her wedding was the happiest day of her life. It was a wonderful feeling to have all the people that mattered the most in her life sharing her special day with her and she too wished that her parents and Howard could have been there. Although it was hard to send Omar Tristan Jones Jr. home with Ms. Bedford, it felt great to finally be alone with her husband.

"It has been said that we should live each day to the fullest but while living each day make memories of the years and 'Don't Waste The Years' because they can sometimes pass by as quickly as the days."

ABOUT THE AUTHOR

WITH MANY DIFFERENT versions of 'Don't Waste the Years' finishing the final chapters has been a dream come true for Lavern Lewis. Who was born in Jamaica and has lived most of her life in Canada. With her passion for writing it has been a long journey for her; to get to where she is today which is an author. She is now promoting her first book and is also working on her next book 'Sinful Thoughts'.

Edwards Brothers Malloy
Thorofare, NJ USA
August 5, 2013